A Smidgen of Sky

A Smidgen of Sky

Dianna Dorisi Winget

HARCOURT CHILDREN'S BOOKS
Houghton Mifflin Harcourt
Boston   New York   2012

Library of Congress Cataloging-in-Publication Data is available.
ISBN 978-0-547-80798-0

Manufactured in the United States of America
DOC 10 9 8 7 6 5 4 3 2 1
4500380779

For Mom and Dad — because you always believed
I could do it

1

"PIPER LEE, HONEY, what do you think of this one?" Mama held up a frilly purple bridesmaid's dress.

I rolled my eyes. "It's great if you want me to look like an eggplant."

Mama made a worried sound under her breath as she sorted through the row of dresses. "Piper Lee, I've shown you fourteen and you've hated every one. Why are you being such a fuss box?"

"Because she's a pain," Ginger said, as if it was some obvious fact.

"Shut up, Ginger."

"You watch your tongue," Mama said. "And you haven't answered my question."

"I'm not trying to be a fuss box, Mama. You just haven't shown me anything I like."

"And what would you like to wear to our wedding—your flight jacket?"

Our wedding? As if I had any say in the matter. As if I were in favor of Mama's changing her name from Heather DeLuna to Mrs. Ben Hutchings. Who'd want to give up a pretty name like DeLuna anyhow? It brought to mind some big, lovely bird soaring through the clouds. But Hutchings? That sounded like a rabbit cage.

Mama said when I grew up and met the right man, I'd be more than happy to take his name. But I wouldn't, not ever. That's on account of my name is special. My daddy named me—Piper Lee DeLuna—exactly six years before he crashed his single-engine Piper Cub into the Atlantic.

Mama turned to Ben. He was sprawled in a brown padded chair in the corner of Crosby's Wedding Shop, his long legs stretched out in front of him and his arms crossed over his white T-shirt. Except for the little smile he gave Mama, he looked like he was napping with his eyes open.

"If you ask me," he said in a soft, deep voice that rolled from his throat, "I think it might be time to make the decision for her."

Ginger clapped her hands. "Let me pick, Daddy. I want

the green one." She whirled back to Mama. "Can we go with the green dress, Heather? I just lo-o-o-ve that one."

I chomped on the inside of my cheek to keep from gagging. *What a weenie.* I'd just as soon roll around in poison oak as get snared with her for a stepsister.

Mama smoothed Ginger's long, blond hair. "I like the green one, too, kiddo." She pulled it off the rack and held it up. "Piper Lee?"

The dress was made of lime-colored shiny stuff on top with a spinach-green skirt. I didn't own anything green except for an olive baseball cap that said FLYING AIN'T JUST FOR BIRDS. "It's so boring, is all," I said.

Ginger smiled as if she were made of molasses. "It would go good with your dark hair."

I fought back the urge to punch her. It was another of those dumb Ginger comments, the kind that made her sound all grown up instead of ten, like me.

Mama pulled two more dresses off the rack—a babyish-looking pink one with white sleeves, and a yellow one the color of what my cat, Mowgli, sometimes spit up on the rug. She held the green dress beside the other two, and her eyebrows shot up. "Okay, these are the three finalists. Which do you hate the least, Piper Lee?"

The pout on Ginger's face told me she didn't think it right I got the final pick. I took my time, watching a frustrated bumblebee bump the store window as it tried to reach the fake hydrangeas on the other side. I finally pointed to a dress still on the rack. "That red one there isn't too bad."

Mama's eyes got real wide. "Oh, Good Friday, Piper Lee."

"What?"

"That wasn't one of your choices," Ben said.

"Well, maybe we ought to look in some other places," I said. "Maybe Savannah or something."

Mama pressed her lips together, building enough steam to bake a sweet potato. "There's no reason to drive fifty miles when we've got perfectly good choices right here. Now, pick a dress."

No way was I picking Ginger's favorite—that left either the pink or the yellow. Did I want to look like a six-year-old or cat spit-up? Which one was Ginger's least favorite? I tried to read her face, like when we played penny poker. It was a gamble, all right. "I guess the pink one."

Ginger's face scrunched. "I don't like that one. Can we please get the green one? Please, Heather?"

Mama fixed Ben with a pleading look. "This is a no-win situation. Help me."

I held my breath. The bumblebee kept bumping the

window. Poor little guy wanted in as badly as I wanted out.

Ben got to his feet. He rubbed a thumb and forefinger over his mustache. "Hmm." He winked at Mama. "I think both girls would look real pretty in the yellow one."

Ginger slapped her legs. *"Da-a-a-d,"* she wailed, loud enough to make one of the store ladies frown in our direction.

Ben cut off Ginger's complaint with a sharp wave of his hand. "Hush, now. You're getting the yellow one, end of story."

Mama wilted with relief.

"I kind of like the yellow one," I told Ginger. "It'll go good with your hair."

She glared at me like a hungry cat eyeing a rat.

Ben chuckled. "Shoot," he said, placing a hand on the back of Ginger's neck. "If I didn't know better, I'd think you girls actually liked each other." Mama clicked her tongue and got a real wishful look in her eyes.

Ben dropped me and Mama off at seven that evening. Together, we trudged up the stairs to our second-floor apartment, the July air so damp and sticky that you could've wrung it out like a washcloth.

"When are we gonna get the air conditioner fixed, Mama?"

"It's not broken, Piper Lee. It just needs to be refilled with coolant."

"So how come you don't just fill it, then?"

"On account of it costs eighty-five dollars. Besides, once we move to Ben's, it won't matter anyway."

"Don't remind me," I muttered. I wiped at the bangs that stuck to my forehead. Nothing sounded as good right then as a dip in the ocean. "Can we go swimming?"

Mama dropped her shopping bag onto the sofa. "Oh, honey, not tonight. We just got home and I'm beat." She reached into the bag from Crosby's and lifted out my yellow dress, smiling at it real sweet. "Here, go hang this up before it gets wrinkled."

"How come Ginger and I couldn't each pick our own dresses, anyhow?"

"You know I want you to match."

"But why? It's not like we're twins."

Mama sighed. "On account of I said so, Piper Lee. We've been through this a million times. Now please just go hang it up like I asked."

"Okay, okay."

Mowgli lay stretched out in the doorway of my room. I took a quick little hop to avoid tripping over him. "Hey, you fat Persian, how you doin', boy?" He sailed up onto my bed and turned his smashed-in face toward me. I giggled. "There you go looking all furious again for no good reason."

I threw the dress beside him and reached for my spray bottle. It sat on my dresser, right below my movie poster for *The Great Waldo Pepper*. I smiled back at Robert Redford and sprayed my neck and arms with water. It was only a poster, but every time I looked at Robert Redford, wearing his brown aviator cap and hanging out of his cockpit, it made me feel as if Daddy were in the room. I flipped on the window fan. It came to life with a roar and I stood right next to it, letting the blast of air blow my hair into a mess.

I stayed there for a couple of minutes cooling off, then turned the fan from high to medium. "Ah, now I feel better. How 'bout you, Mowgli? You feel better now, fat cat?" I glanced over my shoulder and couldn't believe what I saw.

Mowgli was kneading his claws right into the yellow dress.

For a second I just stood there, too stunned to do anything as he worked his big, silky paws up and down. Then I rushed over and grabbed the dress. Snag marks covered the top, with inch-long threads hanging from each one.

"Oh, boy," I whispered, not sure if I should laugh or cry.

"Hey, Piper Lee?"

I shoved the dress into my closet right before Mama stuck her head around the door. "Feel like popcorn? Or are you hungry enough for a TV dinner?"

Good thing for the noisy fan so she couldn't hear my heart pounding. "Um, popcorn sounds good."

Mama left the room, and I pulled the dress out for another look. Fear sloshed in my belly like a bucketful of seawater. I could trim all the loose threads, but how in the world was I supposed to get rid of all the runs? I hung it between my leather flight jacket and my raincoat so the bottom showed but not the top, and I flopped onto the bed beside Mowgli. "I don't like the dress either, but boy, you just got me in boo-coo trouble."

Mama called to let me know supper was ready. I sat beside her on the sofa, munching popcorn and drinking Coke, trying not to fret over the dress.

"I sure do love these easy suppers," Mama said.

"That'll all change if you marry Ben, you know. He'll make you cook all the time."

"And I s'pose he'll lock me in the closet, too."

"He might. He's got some handcuffs."

Mama grinned. "Gee, how unusual for a prison guard. You make him sound like such a tyrant. I thought you liked Ben."

"He's okay. It's Ginger that I can't hardly stand. She's such a brat."

"Yeah? Well, you're not always an angel yourself."

Irritation sizzled through me. That wasn't a very loyal thing for her to say. "Things ought to just stay the way they are. Ben and Ginger can live in their house and we can live in ours, and you can just keep on dating like you have for the past year, and everybody will be happy. Getting married is just . . ."

"Just what, honey?"

"Just wrong, is all."

Mama puffed out her cheeks in a big breath. "Piper Lee, look at me." She waited a second and then reached out and turned my chin toward her. "Your daddy's not coming back."

I pulled away. "You don't know that," I said. "They never found him."

"Don't you think after three solid days of searching, the coast guard would have found him if he'd been any place near the wreckage?"

I'd heard the details of the search a million times.

I knew all about the helicopters and boats and divers. I brushed a hand across my eyes. "Sometimes miracles happen, though."

"That's true enough. That's why I spent three real long years hoping against hope that just maybe he'd come back. Every time the phone rang or somebody who seemed a little familiar came into the Black-eyed Pea, I thought it might be him. But then one day it dawned on me that I had a little girl to raise and a life to live, and I had to stop wishing for the impossible."

"People used to think flying was impossible, but they just hadn't figured out how to do it yet."

I gave a little start as Mama laughed. "Your daddy was a real optimist, too, you know? Just like you."

"He was?"

"You bet. And he was handsome, smart, funny, and brave. But Piper Lee, he wasn't superhuman. There's no way he could have survived that plane crash."

She stopped there. She never added the last little detail of the story. The part about how there might not have been any plane crash if it hadn't been for me. I worked my finger through a hole in the slipcover of the couch. Mama had sewn it a long time ago from some old curtains she'd found at Goodwill.

"But you loved him, right?"

"Yes, course I did."

"How do you know you love Ben?"

Mama's face got all soft and happy. "I just know, honey. Ben's the best thing that's ever happened to me."

I felt a little jab in my heart. There she went being disloyal again. How could Ben be the best thing?

"But you could get along without him if you had to," I said. "We have for a long time."

"I guess. But I don't think I'd want to."

But you could, I thought. *You just said so yourself.*

Mama sent me to bed at ten o'clock, but it was still too hot to sleep. I lay there on top of my covers, fretting over how Mama would skin me alive when she found out about my clawed dress. But then a shaft of moonlight shone across my bed. I looked out my window. I could see only a smidgen of sky, but it was enough to make me think of Daddy. He was my favorite thing to think about before I went to sleep at night. The memories seemed clearest in the quiet and dark.

I remembered how rough and gritty his chin felt when he kissed me good night and how he'd sometimes read to me—Dr. Seuss, or a chapter from one of the Five Little Peppers books, or sometimes a Bible story. I closed my eyes real tight and heard his deep, chuckling laugh. But Ben laughed like that, too. Was I hearing Daddy's laugh or Ben's?

I flipped over, trying to get comfortable. In just two months, if I couldn't find a way to change her mind, Mama would become Mrs. Ben Hutchings and I'd still be Piper Lee DeLuna. Our names wouldn't match anymore. Even our address would change when we moved to Ben's house.

If Daddy came back, how would he ever find us?

2

When I woke up the next morning, my left arm prickled like it was filled with Coke. Mowgli was sprawled across it. I pushed him off with a moan. "Get off, fat cat."

He gave me a disgusted look and then stretched long and slinky, his claws sticking out like little knives. It reminded me of what those little knives had done to my dress. I closed my eyes and yanked the sheet up to try to block out the day, but the sun blasting through the window was too bright. A gentle clackity-clack came from Miss Claudia's sewing machine in the apartment across the hall. I kicked off the covers.

I sniffed the air, wondering if Miss Claudia had made her weekly batch of peach cobbler yet, but all I could smell was perfumy jasmine drifting through the window. Miss Claudia spent all her time doing one of two things — making cobbler and sewing tiny outfits for her two great-grandbabies. She called them her "little slices of heaven." I'd never seen either little slice, since they lived a whole world away in Washington State. But I'd seen plenty of pictures and plenty of sewing patterns.

The sewing machine kept whirring and clacking, whirring and clacking, until a notion tapped its way into my head. I sat up so fast, I scared Mowgli right off the bed.

Miss Claudia! Maybe she could fix my dress. Maybe she'd even agree not to tattle.

"Hey, Mama?" I asked at breakfast. "Can I stay home when you go to work today?"

Mama slid a flapjack onto my plate. "But Ben and Ginger are planning on you."

"Yeah, I know, but I have a whole bunch of clippings I need to glue into my scrapbook."

"Take it with you."

"I can't. It would be a pain to haul it all over there. Besides, I probably couldn't work on it anyhow, on account of Ben always makes us play outside."

Mama raised an eyebrow. "That's a bad thing?"

"Sometimes."

"So work on it later."

I sighed. This was going about the way I'd figured it would. "Why does it matter, Mama? Miss Claudia's always around. She doesn't care if I'm home."

Mama pushed the syrup toward me. "I let you stay home with Miss Claudia most of the time. I don't think having you spend one day a week with Ben and Ginger is too much. You need to spend time together."

About as much as I needed a plateful of slimy okra.

Mama turned back to the griddle and poured another puddle of batter into the spattering oil. "Did you ask Ben about the air show yet?"

"Why can't you ask him? He'll say yes for sure."

"And if you ask?"

"Well, I—I dunno."

She smiled. "You underestimate him, Piper Lee. Ben's a really great guy. If he knows how important the air show is to you, I bet he'll be willing to go."

I swirled a bite of flapjack in my syrup.

"Anyhow," Mama said, "you gotta start sometime."

"Start what?"

"Talking with Ben."

"I talk to him."

"I don't mean one or two words when he asks you a question. I mean a real honest-to-goodness conversation. Like the kind Ginger and I have."

15

"Ginger's just trying to get points."

"Hmm," Mama said. "And all this time I thought she liked me."

"Well, she does like you." I tried to backtrack. "I just think a lot of the stuff she says is to impress you."

"Well, know what I think? I think you underestimate Ginger, too."

I wondered when she'd started liking the word *underestimate* so much. My math teacher talked about using estimates to guess the worth of something. Was Mama saying Ben and Ginger were worth more than I thought they were? A picture of Ginger standing by the side of the road with a FOR SALE sign hanging around her neck made me grin.

"Did I say something funny?" Mama asked.

"No, ma'am."

She winked. "Well, whatever it is, it's nice to see you smile."

We climbed into our old Toyota to head for Ben and Ginger's right after one o'clock. Mama called the car Ol' Faithful on account of we'd had it forever. As soon as we turned onto Hillman Lane, you could see clear down the skinny gravel road to the last place on the left, where Ben and Ginger lived. It wasn't much to look at, a one-story house built of rough gray wood, standing in a yard that was half red dirt and half scrappy lawn. But I liked the patch of sunflowers growing near the porch, the way their huge happy faces seemed to follow the sun across the sky. The big shady area beneath the pecan trees was kind of nice, too.

Ben was tinkering under the hood of his ugly brown Mustang when we pulled into the drive, but as soon as Mama parked the car, he was right there like a hog for his slop. Mama disappeared into his arms. He smiled at me over the top of her head. "Hey, Piper Lee. You come to visit again?"

"Yessir," I said, slurring the two words into one. Mama didn't like when I did that, said it wasn't respectful. She didn't take note. Next time I'd make it more smart-alecky. I sighed real loud as they kissed.

"Ginger's around back on the trampoline," Ben said.

Yahoo for Ginger. "Bye, Mama."

She didn't answer. She was too busy gazing up at Ben as if he were some trophy fish she'd just hooked. I slammed my car door extra hard and wondered when Ben had become more important to her than me.

Before I'd stomped even halfway around the house, I smelled the sharp stink of fingernail polish. I found Ginger sitting cross-legged in the middle of the trampoline, wearing a pink shirt that said "Pep Rally Angel."

Ginger flipped her braid over her shoulder. "Hey, Piper."

"How come you're painting your nails clear?"

"'Cause the glitter looks the most silvery that way."

She picked up a small tube and dusted it over the wet polish. "See?" She waved a shimmering hand toward me. "Want some?"

I wrinkled my nose. "No."

"How come? It's pretty."

"It's dog ugly."

"You're dog ugly."

"At least I don't wear a size-seven shoe," I snapped back, but even as I said it, I knew I was mad at Mama and not Ginger.

Ginger screwed the cap back onto the tube of glitter. I crawled into the shade under the trampoline, yanked a long blade of grass, and stuck it into the side of my mouth.

"A dog probably peed on that," Ginger said, peering down.

"You don't have a dog."

"Neighbor dog, maybe."

I heard Mama start up Ol' Faithful. It roared all the way down Hillman Lane before the silence closed in. Stuck again. "So what do you want to do today?"

"Swimming sounds good."

I perked up a little. "Can we?"

"Hey, Daddy," Ginger called. "When you get through with the car, can you take us swimming?"

His answer drifted back with the breeze. "I s'pose so."

Ginger smiled, but right then I remembered I didn't have my swimming suit with me. "Oh, shoot. My suit's at home."

"I'll find you some shorts," she said.

The thought of wearing Ginger's stuff made me feel weird, but I did want to go swimming. "Yeah, okay."

"But first I have to practice this cheer once more."

"You know, by the time you get in high school, the cheers are gonna be different."

She bounced to her feet. "So?"

I covered my ears.

"Gimme an *A*. Gimme a *B*. Gimme a real *VIC-TOR-Y*."

The trampoline stretched down real low by my head. I scrambled out from underneath just in time.

A few minutes later we trooped upstairs to Ginger's bedroom. She dug a pair of yellow shorts and a halter top out of her dresser. "These okay?"

The yellow shorts made me think about my bridesmaid's dress. "Yeah. Thanks."

Ginger peeled off her shirt. She had on one of those training bras I'd seen in the J. C. Penney catalog—white, with a tiny butterfly in the middle. "Where'd you get that?"

"Bought it with my allowance."

"Does your daddy know?"

"Not yet."

I studied my nubby fingernails. I wanted to ask more about it without acting too interested. I didn't have much need for a bra yet. Then again, Ginger didn't either. I'd ask Mama about getting me one. I scooped up the shorts and halter top and headed for the bathroom.

An hour later the three of us were on our way to Glen Bay Beach. I'd been there only a few times. Mama and I usually went to the main swimming beach at Shady Hollow. But I liked Glen Bay better—it had the little island.

Ben parked the truck near a big mass of saltwort on the edge of the shore. I left my shoes in the cab and slid out, loving the gritty feel of sand between my toes. We walked over to about twenty feet from the water and spread out our beach towels.

Ben pulled his T-shirt over his head and headed for the water. As if on second thought, he turned toward us and took a couple of steps backwards. "Y'all stick right close to shore, you hear?"

I sifted a little pile of sand onto each corner of my towel in case a gust of wind tried to grab it. Ginger plunked down onto hers. "You still wearing that training bra?" I asked.

"No, silly. You don't wear a bra with a swimming suit."

My face got hot. "I knew that. I just wondered, is all."

"Bet you didn't know boys' swim trunks have the underwear built right in."

"I guess you figured that out when you bought yourself a pair."

She wrinkled her nose at me and stretched out on her towel.

"Aren't you gonna swim?" I asked.

"Yeah, but I have to lie here in the sun and get real hot first or else the water's too cold."

"Don't be such a weenie. It's practically lukewarm."

I raised a hand to shield my eyes and studied the island. It wasn't a real island, just a big mound not far from the beach, covered with saltwort and scrub grass. There were five older kids doing crazy jumps and dives off a giant round floatie thing next to the island. I wanted to swim out there, but I wasn't allowed. Mama said I wasn't a strong enough swimmer to go much over my head.

But Mama wasn't here.

Ben swam in the opposite direction, his long, powerful strokes gliding him away from us. Ginger was flopped on her back, an arm thrown across her eyes.

I walked over to the edge of the water and stuck my toes in. My whole body prickled with sudden excitement. I took a deep breath of salty air and squinted out over the Atlantic, clear out to where the brilliant blue of the sky seemed to blend right into the blue of the water. Daddy had crashed into this very ocean, only about fifteen miles from where I stood.

All at once I didn't care if Mama thought I wasn't a strong swimmer or if Ben had said to stick close to shore. With a shiver, I dove in and headed for the island.

3

I TOOK OFF swimming hard and furious, feeling all proud of myself. I'd swim out, touch that island, and circle back before anybody even missed me. I kept up a steady pace as long as I could, resisting the urge to look back. After a while, though, my arms started to burn, and I stopped to get my bearings. I couldn't believe it. The darn island had moved way off to my left. It didn't look much closer than it had from the beach. I figured I should turn around. I almost wanted to. But for some crazy reason, I kept paddling, glancing up every few seconds to keep a straight course.

Fear of drowning was about all that kept me going,

because by the time I finally reached the island, my arms were so dead that I couldn't even haul myself out of the water. I grabbed hold of a big bunch of scrub grass and hung on till my heart slowed a bit and I could finally muster the strength to climb into the mess of weeds.

The kids on the floatie were playing around, making as much ruckus as a bunch of stuck pigs. Nobody said anything to me, but I could tell by their looks that they didn't figure I had any right to invade their privacy.

I spotted Ben. He'd looped around and was swimming toward Ginger, who was still stretched out on the beach like a catfish ready to fry. I shivered. A red-haired boy took a flying leap off the floatie, pulling his knees up to his chest in midair. Then one of the girls jumped, too, but she did it real sissylike—feet first, holding her nose. I figured that's how Ginger would jump.

Ben was almost back to shore.

I bit my lip, not sure why swimming out to the island had seemed like such a great idea. I tried to rub some feeling back into my numb arms and took a couple of long, slow breaths. The sun felt so good. If I could only nap for a minute or two, I'd be good as new. But no sooner did I close my eyes than one of the girls said, "Hey, kid, your daddy's calling you."

I raised my head. A girl in a pink bikini balanced on the edge of the floatie. She pointed toward the beach. Ben was treading water halfway between the shore and the island.

My nose filled with the awful stinging that comes right before tears.

"It's okay," I said. "He's not my daddy." Without giving myself another second to think about it, I slipped into the water.

My arm muscles started to holler right away. I did my best to ignore them and just concentrate on breathing, but the swells spattered droplets into my nose and I sputtered and coughed.

Don't be a weenie, I commanded myself. *It's not as far as it looks.* But as hard as I kicked and flailed toward shore, it seemed to stay just about as far away. Then my left shoulder cramped, and the blazing pain made me panic.

I looked for Ben. A big splash of water smacked me in the face. *This is it,* I thought. *I'm gonna disappear right here in the Atlantic, just like Daddy.*

But then there came a new sound—a loud voice, right close to my ear. Ben bobbed beside me. "This way," he said. "Swim with me."

"I can't," I gasped. "Can't."

"Course you can." He took hold of my cramped arm.

The pain blasted clear down to the tips of my fingers and nearly brought me right up out of the water. It was like being stabbed with a needle.

Ben towed me several feet before he let go. "Now swim. You're almost there."

Instinct took over. My hands slapped, my feet kicked. And finally, I felt sand under my feet.

I stopped in chest-deep water, wheezing for air, sure my pounding heart was gonna blow right out of my skin. As soon as I could raise my arms, I rubbed the stinging salt water from my eyes, and the world came back into focus. I felt like laughing—I was so happy to be alive.

But then I caught a sideways glimpse of Ben towering beside me, his hair dripping and his wide shoulders pumping up and down with each breath.

Goose bumps sprang up all over me. I knew I needed to say something, but what? *Sorry I ignored you? Thanks for saving my life? Please don't beat me half to death?* I don't remember even thinking the question that did pop out of my mouth. "Are you gonna tell Mama 'bout this?"

His expression could've toasted a marshmallow. He pointed to my towel and said, "Go. Sit." I slunk out of the water feeling like a whipped pup.

Ginger's eyes were huge. "Man, Piper. You're crazy as a bedbug. You darn near drowned."

"Did not," I said.

Ginger looked at Ben. "She could've. Huh, Daddy?"

I collapsed onto my towel and wondered if there was any way I could keep him from telling Mama. As if letting Mowgli claw my dress wasn't bad enough. Now this.

Nobody spoke for a month of Sundays.

I tilted my head to drain the last of the water out of my ear.

About the time my arms started to feel like a part of me again, Ginger stood and stretched. "Okay, I'm gonna go get cooled off now. You coming, Piper?"

Before I even had a chance to consider, Ben said, "Piper's gonna sit a spell."

Ginger screwed up her face, but for once she kept her mouth shut. She just stood there, wiggling her toes in the sand, then headed for the water.

Wait, I wanted to call after her. *Don't leave me here alone with your daddy.* But that's just what she did.

Ben still looked as hot as the pepper sauce Mama liked to sprinkle on her greens.

I sat up and pulled my knees close to my chest to try to muffle the thumping of my heart. I'd never been all alone with Ben before.

I studied the sand clumped on my toes and looked at the giant white magnolia on my beach towel, all while I kept a nervous watch on Ben out of the corner of my eye. His hair was brown and full and kicked up a little at the neck. I could tell from his tan exactly how far the sleeves went down on his prison-guard uniform.

I inched over to the far side of my beach towel, but it didn't feel nearly far enough. Right about the time I thought I might explode from worry, there it was, high up above: the thin contrail of a jet. A perfect white chalk mark against the indigo sky. "I know what causes those," I blurted.

My comment hung in the air like the trail from the plane. I wondered if Ben had even heard me. But after a few seconds his head tilted up to where I was looking. "That right?"

"Yeah. The air is real cold way up there, at least forty below zero. When the jet burns fuel, it releases water vapor that freezes right away. So the vapor looks like a thin white line."

"Sounds like you've done your homework."

The awful silence started to close in on us again. "Do you like airplanes?" I asked in desperation.

"I like 'em when they're on time."

"Well—have you ever been to an air show?"

"Seen a couple over the years."

I swallowed, encouraged by the way his voice had lightened a bit. Maybe I could talk him out of being mad at me. "Well, they're really cool. There's going to be one round here in a couple weeks. A real big one."

"Is that so?"

"Yeah. In Savannah. The Blue Angels are gonna be there. You know, the United States Navy performers who fly the F/A-Eighteen Hornets?"

"Uh-huh."

Ask him if he wants to go, I heard Mama whisper in my ear. *Ask him now.* But I couldn't get my tongue to form the words.

I traced one of the magnolia petals on my towel. "Thanks for . . . for helping me out there."

Ben turned cool eyes on me. "The ocean's a mighty thing. You gotta respect it."

"Yes, sir."

The end of the jet contrail was flat and gauzy now, kind of like cotton candy.

"So, um, are you gonna tell Mama about this?"

He didn't answer right away; his eyes still followed the jet. Then he leaned back onto his elbows and said,

"Keeping secrets doesn't do much good for a relationship, but I don't s'pose she'd care if we talked about airplanes behind her back."

It took me a second to register his meaning. I should've been glad—thankful, even. But it wasn't really what I'd been expecting. Why would he take my side? A weird tickly feeling in my belly told me to stand guard.

4

As soon as Mama left for work the next day, I grabbed my bridesmaid's dress and hurried across the hall. I'd been hearing the rattle of Miss Claudia's sewing machine all morning.

"Come on in," she called when I knocked.

I peeked around her door with a smile. "Hey, it's just me."

She grinned. Woolly white hair sprang out from beneath the soft felt cap she wore. "'Jus' me'? Well, bless your heart, child. I can't think of a visitor I'd rather have."

She always greeted me as if I were famous, even if

she'd seen me earlier in the day. It got a little embarrassing, but it also made me feel special.

"What are you working on today?" I asked as I padded across the braided rug covering most of her living room floor.

"Well, now, I'm just finishing up a vest. For my new little great-grandbaby, you know. I told you about him, right?"

"Oh, yes, ma'am. You've told me all about Jeffrey McAllister the third."

She held up a sewing pattern and pointed to the model's tiny tan-checkered vest. "Don't you think he'll look jus' like a little gentleman in this, all shined and spiffed up?"

I didn't think a two-month-old baby could look much like a gentleman no matter what he wore, but I nodded. "That's real nice, Miss Claudia."

She tipped her head to peer over her glasses. "What you got there, Piper Lee? It looks awful pretty."

I unfolded the dress and held it up.

"Well, if that isn't the most gorgeous thing. That's for your mama's wedding, now, isn't it? I was wondering when you were gonna get over here to . . ." She leaned closer. "My goodness, child. What happened to it?"

"It was Mowgli. I just laid it on the bed for a minute, and he clawed it."

A whistle sliced the air. "Well, my goodness. I bet your mama took a switch to both of you."

"Not yet. She doesn't know. Can you help me fix it before she finds out?"

"What? You think ol' Miss Claudia's gonna help you fool your mama?"

"I was hoping maybe."

Her cheeks pushed way up high, and she chuckled. "Well, we can't have your mama upset at you, now, can we? You go get yourself some peach cobbler and milk, and I'll see what I can do with this dress."

I let out my breath in a big, noisy puff. "That'd be great."

She pushed away from the sewing machine with a groan and shuffled over to her ironing board. She stretched the dress out and leaned over so close, I expected her glasses to slide right off the end of her nose. "My, my. What are we gonna do here?"

I poured myself a glass of milk, dished up some cobbler, and sat at the kitchen table where I could keep an eye on Miss Claudia. She squinted at my dress for so long, I worried maybe she couldn't fix it. But then she reached for her sewing shears and started clipping loose threads.

"So when is this wedding, again, Piper Lee?"

"Two months."

"Ahh. I bet you're jus' as excited as can be."

"Not really," I said through a mouthful of cobbler. "Me and Mama are just fine like we are."

You'd think I had let loose with a string of swear words for how quiet it got. Miss Claudia stopped snipping.

I stopped chewing.

"Don't you love your mama, Piper Lee?" Miss Claudia finally asked.

"Well, course I do."

"Then you should be tickled pink that she's lucky enough to find somebody to care for. Don't you know the Good Book there says you gotta treat people the way you wanna be treated?"

An old Bible lay near me on the table, its gold letters scuffed and worn from years of loving use. I swore it was glaring at me.

"Well, yes, ma'am. It's just that Ginger and I don't get along much. She only likes Mama." I knew it was weak, but it was all that came to me right then.

"Well, course she likes your mama, fine woman that she is. Girls need a mama. Poor little thing's never had one, has she?"

I tried to recall the little bits of information I'd heard. "I know her name was Tina, and she left when Ginger was a baby."

"There you go," Miss Claudia declared, as if that explained everything. "She's probably jealous as all get out."

Jealous? Ginger was a spoiled brat and got too many A's on her report card. But jealous? Of me?

"You jus' wait and see," Miss Claudia said. "The four of you are gonna be as happy as a rooster in a hen house." She pointed to a little plastic bin on her sewing table. "Could you bring that to me, child?"

I carried it over, glad for the distraction. She popped the lid, and her chocolate fingers rummaged through a bunch of sewing odds and ends—thimbles and half-used spools of thread, buttons, little bits of fabric and lace. She pulled out a small white tube and held it out to me. "This here is fabric glue. You watch, now—this is magic."

"But it's white!" I cried as she squeezed out the first strip.

"No, no, not to fret, now. As soon as it dries, it'll be clear and it'll pull the fabric together. It won't be perfect, but nobody will notice."

I bit my bottom lip as she squeezed out six more strips, each about an inch long. Then, magically, the first strip began to turn clear, and I let out a happy breath. "Hey, that's lookin' pretty good."

"See? What did I tell you?"

It was another ten minutes before my dress was dry. Miss Claudia put it on a pretty padded hanger and sent me home.

Mowgli lay in a tight ball at the end of my bed, one paw over his eyes, as if he were trying to block the sun.

"Hey, fat cat. Check out my dress. It's still ugly, but it looks good as new."

I whomped my hand onto the pillow to get his attention. Dust particles twirled up my nose and made me sneeze, but the shocked look on Mowgli's face was worth it. "You deserved that for causing me all this trouble."

I hung the dress in my closet. One problem out of the way. But Robert Redford smiling down at me made me think of Daddy, and I realized that fixing the dress hadn't

36

really solved anything at all. I flopped down next to Mowgli and thought about the day Mama had met Ben. She'd come home from her shift at the Black-eyed Pea with leftover biscuits and gravy for our supper, her face all pink and happy.

Mama definitely smiled more now and looked prettier. She even sang as she did stuff around the house. Those were nice things. But then I noticed my fifth-grade school picture on the bookshelf. It reminded me of another picture, my favorite one in the world.

I got my aviation scrapbook off my dresser. Daddy grinned out at me from a big newspaper clipping, his Piper Cub parked a few feet behind him. The picture was taken the day he was awarded a silver plaque for his flawless ten-year safety record taking aerial photographs for the Georgia Board of Tourism.

Mama had clipped five newspaper articles about Daddy—this one about the award and the other four about the accident—and had given them to me when I'd started the scrapbook.

I laid my school picture beside the grinning photo of Daddy, comparing our faces the way I'd done a hundred times before. We had the same chestnut hair—thick and with a mind all of its own. Mama said we had the same smile. I couldn't be sure; I looked pretty serious in my school picture. The longer I compared them, the more the photos blurred together. I wiped at my eyes.

"Daddy," I whispered. "I am so sorry I kept you from going up to look for those people earlier."

5

I MUST HAVE fallen asleep, for the next thing I heard was Mama's key jiggling the lock. I sat up and stretched, trying to shake off the sleepy feeling as I stumbled out to the living room.

Mama struggled through the door, balancing her purse and two overloaded grocery bags. "Hey, kiddo."

"Hey, Mama. Today's not grocery day."

"No, but Ben and Ginger are coming for supper tonight. Did you forget?"

Oh, yahoo. "I don't remember you telling me."

Mama kicked off her loafers and handed me one of the bags.

I peeked inside. "No okra in here, I hope."

"Nope. I thought we'd just fry up some chicken and have corn bread and salad with it. Nothin' too fancy. Oh, shoot. I forgot to buy buttermilk."

I knew what she was thinking. Ginger hated corn bread without buttermilk to pour on top. I hid my smile. "Oh, well," I said.

Supper was supposed to be at five thirty, but Ben and Ginger didn't show up. Mama set the chicken in the oven to keep it warm. It smelled so good, I could hardly stand it. By ten to six my belly rumbled like thunder. I kept picking little bits of tomato and celery off the salad.

They finally showed up at six thirty. Ben was still wearing his tan prison-guard uniform, and his hair was rumpled. I'd never seen him look so tired. He ducked his head to give Mama a kiss. "Sorry, y'all," he said.

Ginger wore shorts and a pink tank top that said "Miss Kitty" across the front. I wondered if she was wearing that training bra again. I still needed to talk to Mama about getting me one.

Mama gave Ben the once-over, reaching up to smooth his hair. "What happened, guy? Rough day?"

"Somethin' like that."

"Wanna talk about it?"

"No, ma'am. I'm starved."

"Me too," I said. "Supper's been ready for—" Mama shot me a look, and I shut my mouth.

Ginger caught the look and giggled. "What's that, Piper?"

"Mama made corn bread, but we're outta buttermilk."

Her face turned into a big wrinkle. "Piper Lee, that is not what you were gonna say."

"Hey," Ben warned. "I'm not in the mood, so don't even start."

Ginger narrowed her eyes at me from behind his back.

I clamped my lips real tight to keep a giggle from slipping out.

Mama carried the chicken and corn bread over to the table and set out some beer and Cokes before sliding into the chair next to Ben's.

"Could you pass me a Coke, please, Heather?" Ginger said.

"I'll take a beer," I said.

Mama handed each of us a cherry Coke.

Ben said a ten-second blessing, and nobody spoke again till we'd polished off most of supper. Then Ben took a

41

long swig of his beer and said, "The inmates caught wind of the governor's new bill today."

Mama dabbed at her mouth with a napkin. "The one that cuts the budget for some of the prison programs?"

"Cuts the prison library hours in half and gets rid of most of the sports programs, too."

"So, was there a lot of ruckus?"

"Oh, yeah. Kenny and I dragged three guys to solitary over it; that was just from my unit."

"How come prisoners get to play sports, anyhow?" I said. "I thought prison was to punish you."

Ben took another long sip of beer and wiped his mouth with the back of his hand. "Diversion, mostly. You've got seven hundred guys locked up—they need some way to burn energy."

"I guess it's understandable they wouldn't be real happy about it," Mama said. "Do you expect more trouble over it?"

Ben raised his eyebrows and said nothing.

"You keep talking about guys," I said. "Aren't there any ladies?"

Ben smirked. "Well, *ladies* don't usually end up in prison, but no, there aren't any women inmates where I work."

Seven hundred prisoners. That seemed like a whole lot to handle, especially if they were all upset about something. It made me wonder if Ben ever got scared. I was about to ask him when I noticed Ginger eyeing the last chicken leg.

We both reached for it at the same time. "I only had two," I said.

"You did not. You had three."

"Like you were keeping track."

"No, I just saw, is all. Daddy and you had three, and me and Mama had . . ."

I was so surprised, I let go of the drumstick. Ginger's eyes got as big as Mowgli's food bowl. Even Ben and Mama seemed stunned for a second. Then Mama got this goofy little smile on her face and winked at Ginger.

Ben took the chicken leg from Ginger, pulled off the meat as best he could, and gave us each half. "There. Now nobody has any reason to bellyache."

Ginger's face turned the color of a ripe watermelon. She picked up her meat and nibbled at it. I did the same.

"Come on," Mama said to Ben. "You look like you could use a neck rub."

"Mmm. Be a fool to turn down an offer like that."

"Would you girls please put the dishes in the dish-washer?" Mama said, leading Ben into the living room.

I waited until they disappeared before whispering, "She's not your mama, you know."

Ginger didn't look up. "I know. It just slipped out, is all."

I wanted to warn her not to ever slip again or I'd slap her silly, but there was something in her voice that made me bite my tongue. I heard Miss Claudia say, *"Girls need a mama,"* just as clear as if she were leaning over my shoulder.

I picked up a piece of chicken skin and stretched it until it snapped.

Ginger moved a little piece of corn bread away from her salad.

"So, speaking about mamas," I said, taking a chance, "what happened to yours, anyhow?"

"She left when I was a baby."

"How come?"

"I dunno. Daddy says they got married too young."

"How old was she?"

"Nineteen."

Nineteen sounded plenty grown up. "You know anything about her?"

"I've seen pictures. She's real pretty. Daddy says I look a lot like her. He says she was real nice and popular, too. She was on the drill team."

I didn't understand how somebody could be nice and yet walk out on her own kid. And if age had been the problem, how come she hadn't come back? Wasn't she curious to see how Ginger was turning out? "Do you know where she's at now?"

"No. But she called from Colorado on my sixth birthday and left a message on the answering machine."

"Colorado? You mean she went and turned Yankee?" I could tell Ginger didn't think it was funny, and I felt kind of bad for teasing. "So what did the message say?"

"Just that she'd call back later. But she didn't."

"Probably chickened out."

Ginger's mouth turned into a square of anger. "You don't know that."

"Don't go getting all in a flap. I only meant it would be hard to be gone for a long time and then just call like that." I lowered my voice to a whisper. "Have you ever thought about trying to find her?"

Ginger screwed her face up like I'd asked the question in Chinese. I fully expected her to tell me I didn't have a speck of brains. But she just sat there, her mouth half-open, looking like a real doofus. Then she whispered, "How would I do that?"

I eased back in my chair and took a long, slow look out to the living room to buy myself a few seconds to think. Then I hunched toward Ginger and said the first thing that jumped into my head. "Well, I s'pose the phone book would be a good place to start."

6

"Which phone book?" Ginger said. "She don't live around here."

"Are you sure? Maybe she moved back."

"To the coast?"

"Well, maybe not right here. Maybe Oakdale or Atlanta or someplace."

Ginger shook her head. "I don't think she lives in Georgia, Piper. She called from Colorado, 'member?"

"We could look on the Internet."

"We don't have the Internet."

"No. But the library does. Has a bunch of phone books, too, I think."

She scowled. For a few minutes I'd really had her going, but now she looked more put-out than interested.

"Her last name is Hutchings, right?"

"I don't think so. Daddy said her name was Liman."

"Okay, hold on." I scooted back my chair. Mama was perched on the edge of the big recliner, rubbing Ben's neck. He sat on the rug in front of her, his eyes closed while they chatted.

I tiptoed over to the kitchen counter and pulled the phone book from its drawer.

Ginger watched with narrowed eyes. "This isn't gonna work, Piper."

"Don't know till you try," I said, borrowing one of Mama's favorite lines.

I sat beside her and opened the book to the white pages. At first we couldn't find anyone with the name of Liman. But then Ginger said maybe it was *L-y* and not *L-i*. Changing the spelling worked. She stopped running her finger down the page and sucked in her breath. "Here's two of them."

My heart pumped faster. I hadn't expected there to be any. "Yeah? Where?"

"Here. Rebecca M. Lyman and Francis Lyman." Ginger slumped. "But Mama's name is Tina. These guys aren't her."

48

"Oh," I said. "Maybe they know her. Shoot, they're probably your relatives."

Ginger and I hunched back over the book, as if staring at the names might answer our questions. She twirled a section of hair around her finger and unrolled it just as fast.

"Maybe the next time your daddy's busy outside, you could try calling these numbers," I said.

"And say what?"

"Well, you could, um, say something like 'I'm looking for Tina Lyman and wondered if you might know her.'"

Ginger's eyebrows scrunched. I could tell she wanted to believe me but wouldn't let herself.

"What are you girls whispering about?" Ben called out from the living room.

Ginger jumped so hard, she banged her leg into the table.

We both whirled around just as Mama and Ben walked into the kitchen.

Ben grinned. "Shoot," he said. "You two look as guilty as Pedro Wooly when I caught him with a fork from the cafeteria."

Mama giggled.

"Pedro Wooly? Is he a person or a sheep?" I asked, my nerves still on high alert.

"Hard to tell," Ben said. "Looks a little like both."

I groped for the front of the phone book and flipped it shut.

Ginger still stared. She looked real guilty, all right.

"So what are you up to?" Mama asked.

"Nothing," I said. "I was just showing Ginger something."

Mama and Ben exchanged a look.

For once Ginger did the helpful thing. She stood and carried the phone book back to the drawer. I started stacking supper plates and humming "Ode to Billie Joe."

"Well," Mama said, "we came to tell you there's a fifties car show going on at the park. We thought we might go stroll around for a bit after you girls get the kitchen done."

"Oh, okay," I said. "Be done in a minute."

Charlesburg Park swarmed with folks eating hot dogs and boiled peanuts, oohing and aahing over the old cars. Some of the ladies wore pink poodle skirts or rolled-up jeans and white T-shirts. I thought they looked like weenies, but I liked the '50s music blaring through the park. The cars were okay, too—not as great as airplanes, but still pretty cool, splashed with shiny chrome and shimmering paint.

Soon Ginger started holding her hair up off her neck and complaining she was too hot, but I was glad we'd come. The air smelled of barbecued pork and mowed grass and the fishy scent of the Atlantic.

Ben stopped in front of a sleek silver Mustang. He gave an admiring whistle. "This is how mine's gonna look one day."

I had my doubts about that. The ugly brown Mustang parked in his yard didn't look anything like this one.

Mama smiled. "In a few more years and with a few more dollars."

"You know," Ben said, "if you'd let me take an early retirement, I'd have a lot more time to work on it."

"I hate to tell you this, guy, but you got another twenty years before you can take early retirement."

"Well, shoot," he said. "That's not what I wanted to hear."

Mama giggled her little-girl laugh, the laugh she saved just for Ben. I couldn't help but notice how happy she seemed, strolling beside him, holding his hand. But it was Daddy's hand she should've been holding, not Ben's.

"Hey, Piper." Ginger nudged me. "Looky there." A little kid ambled past with a huge ice cream. It was melting faster than he could eat it, leaving brown ribbons of chocolate streaming down his wrist.

"Want to get some?" Ginger asked.

I nodded.

Ginger hopped up beside Ben. "Hey, Daddy? Can I get some ice cream?"

Ben didn't answer. He was still drooling over the silver Mustang. Ginger darted around in front of him, wrapped her arms around his waist, and stepped right up on his toes.

"Hey," he said with a fake scowl. "Get off my feet."

"I need some ice cream."

"You do, huh? Well, goody for you. Now get off my feet."

"No, sir. I think I'll stay right here until you give me some money."

Ben smirked. "Then I guess you got another think coming." He scooped her up under the arms and dropped her beside him.

"Hey," she squealed. "No fair."

My throat burned hot and tight. Mama was into hugs and pats and stuff. But it sure would be fun to have a daddy to roughhouse with.

An old lady in a straw hat watched us from the next row of cars. She wore a dopey smile, as if Ben and Ginger horsing around was the cutest thing she'd ever seen. It reminded me of Miss Claudia's face when she talked about her great-grandbabies.

The old lady looked from Ginger to me, and I could read what she was thinking just as plain as if it were stamped on her wrinkled face. She thought Mama and Ben were married and Ginger and I were their kids.

And for just a second, I wished it were true.

But then I thought of Daddy. I owed it to him to set that old lady straight, to tell her she had it all wrong. That Ginger wasn't my sister and Ben wasn't my daddy. That my daddy had been an Air Force pilot and not just a prison guard.

But of course I didn't say anything. I just glanced down, and it felt as though somebody had jabbed me in the chest with a sharp stick.

Ben reached into his back pocket for his wallet. He pulled out four one-dollar bills. "This is all I've got, so if it costs more than this, you're out of luck."

He offered two of the bills to Ginger and the other two to me. Ginger grabbed hers.

I squirmed, staring at the money. It would've been okay if Mama had offered it, but I just couldn't take it from Ben. After all, going to buy ice cream was the very last thing Daddy and I had done together. I took a step back. "That's okay. I'm still full from supper." I fumbled with the hem on my shorts.

"You sure?" Ben asked.

No, I wanted to say, *I'm not sure about anything.* But I just said, "Yes, sir, I'm sure."

Ginger wrinkled up her nose. "You don't got a speck of brains, Piper Lee."

I turned my back on Mama and Ben. Ginger sped off through the crowd toward the ice cream stand and returned a few minutes later with a giant scoop of strawberry swirl. It looked so good, I could hardly stand it. I wanted to grab it and splat it in her face.

"Mmm," Ben said. "I think I need some of that. Want to share a scoop with me, Heather?"

"I don't know. I'm supposed to be watching my figure."

"Oh, come on, now," he said. "That's my job."

Mama giggled. "You and your sweet talk, Ben Hutchings." She winked at me as Ben pulled her off toward the ice cream stand. "Be right back, honey."

I shrugged. Ginger found a shady spot behind an old Chevy to sit. I tried to act interested in the Chevy, but the tears in my eyes made it too blurry to see.

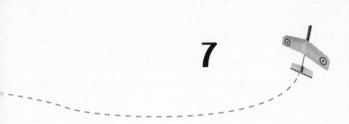

7

IT TOOK ME three days of brainstorming to come up with what I named "Operation Finding Tina." The details took another two days. But by late Sunday night I'd boiled the whole thing down to two simple steps.

Step one: find Tina. Step two: convince Ginger to call her.

Things would just happen natural-like after that. Ginger and Tina would talk, and then Tina would come to visit. She'd realize what she was missing out on, that she never should've left in the first place, that she still loved Ben. The two of them would get back together. Mama and Ben would cancel their wedding.

I grinned into the darkness as Mowgli purred beside me. It was a perfect plan—as slick as spitting watermelon seeds. How come I hadn't thought of it sooner?

The only downside was Mama—she'd be pretty disappointed. But I knew she'd be okay. She'd still have me. And I'd find some way to make her feel better.

"Mama, can I ride my bike to the library?" I asked the next morning.

Mama gave up her struggle to open a plastic bag of Toasty O's and reached for the scissors. "The library? By your lonesome?"

"It's only a couple miles."

"But you've never done it alone."

"I can do it, Mama. I'm not a baby, you know."

"I never said you were. I'm just not comfortable with you riding around downtown by yourself yet."

I clamped my teeth. Getting to the library was supposed to be the easy part. "How old do I have to be?"

"What's going on? You act like you're all put-out with me."

"No. I just think I should be able to ride to the dumb library by myself."

Mama sighed. She tipped the bag of cereal and poured herself a bowl. "Tell you what—tonight after work, we'll swing by the library 'fore we come home. That good enough?"

I dug my nails into my palms. I didn't want to put off Operation Finding Tina for another minute. But if I acted too restless and eager, Mama would get suspicious. "I guess."

"Great. So what do you and Ginger have planned for this afternoon?"

"Oh, let's see. She'll probably try to talk me into painting my toenails. Then she'll want me to listen to a hundred stupid cheers. And then who knows."

Mama clucked her tongue. "Oh, Piper Lee."

"Well, it's true," I said. "That's the kind of stuff she likes."

"And have you ever thought about trying to share some of your interests with her? How about taking your scrapbook over and showing it to her?"

"She doesn't care anything about airplanes."

"You assume that. How do you really know?"

"I just do, Mama."

"Maybe. Or maybe it's a case of not being able to see the orchard for the fruit trees." I had absolutely no idea what that meant.

After breakfast I carried my scrapbook to the kitchen

table along with a bunch of loose clippings. One of the clippings was about the Aero Flight School in Atlanta. As long as you could pass a physical exam, you could start flying lessons at sixteen years old. In just more than five years I'd be old enough. I mentioned that to Mama as she wiped down the countertops.

"Mmm," is all she said.

"What's that mean?" I asked.

"It doesn't mean anything, Piper Lee. I just don't want you to get your hopes up too high. I bet flying lessons are real expensive."

"Thirty-eight dollars an hour for the instructor and about sixty an hour to rent a plane."

"Oh, Good Friday."

"It's okay," I told her. "I'll be old enough to get a job by then. I'll pay for everything myself."

She stepped over and kissed the top of my head. "Let's worry about it when the time comes. Okay?"

I felt like reaching up and rubbing that kiss away. "Daddy would want me to do it."

"Your daddy would want you to follow your own dream, not necessarily his."

She didn't get it. "But Mama, I am. That's what I am doing."

As we drove to Ben's that afternoon, I tried to decide if I should tell Ginger about Operation Finding Tina or wait until I'd made it to the library. By the time we reached Hillman Lane, I'd decided to wait. As badly as I wanted to blurt it out, I worried she'd ask questions I couldn't answer yet and maybe ruin the whole plan.

We pulled into the driveway, and the roar of the lawn mower greeted us. Ben pushed it around the corner of the house and released the handle. The engine died with an angry sputter.

I gave Mama a quick hug before Ben could reach her. "See ya," I said. Then I escaped into the house so I didn't have to watch them kiss and carry on as though they hadn't seen each other in a year.

I went over to Ginger's room. Her door was closed.

"Hey," I said. "Knock, knock."

No answer. I tapped on the door. "Hey, Ginger?"

"Go away."

I let my fist drop to my side. "Do what?"

"You heard me. Just go away."

I waited, staring at the poster of beagle puppies taped to her door, not sure what to do. If she wouldn't let me in her room, what in the world was I supposed to do all afternoon? Hang out with Ben?

"I don't have anywhere to go away to," I said.

She didn't answer.

I hesitated a few seconds longer. Then I took a deep breath and opened her door a crack. She lay curled up like a snail shell, her back to me.

"Hey, what's wrong? Are you mad at me or something?"

She flipped over and scowled at me, her eyes red and puffy. "I don't want to find my mama, Piper. She doesn't want anything to do with me."

I felt as if she'd thrown a bucket of ice water on me. "W-why do you think that? You try to call one of those phone numbers or something?"

She sniffed and rubbed a hand across her eyes. "No. I thought maybe Daddy had her number, but then I found this." She pulled an envelope from underneath her pillow.

All my senses sprang to full alert. I stepped into the room and closed her door behind me.

"It's a letter that Mama wrote to Daddy before she left us."

"Where did you get it?"

She sat up. "I found it in Daddy's box."

"What box?"

"His safety box, where he keeps important stuff like insurance papers and birth certificates and stuff like that.

There were a couple other letters, too, from when he and Mama were dating. But this one . . . you can read it if you want."

I drew back like she'd offered me a handful of poison oak. "That's okay. I better not."

"No. Go ahead. I don't care."

I couldn't believe she was willing to share something so personal with me, especially something that wasn't any of my business. "Ginger, I don't think I should."

She threw the envelope at my feet. "Shut up and read it, Piper Lee."

I swallowed.

She watched until I bent down and picked up the letter, and then she curled up like a snail again.

I sat on the edge of her bed to read.

Dear Ben,
I hope you don't hate me for
this. I know you probably will.
But I just can't live like this
anymore. I thought I was ready
to settle down, but I guess
I'm not, because each day I
feel like I'm going crazy. You
don't know what it's like to be

stuck at home with a baby every day. She cries so much. It's really, really hard. I didn't want to be a mother yet. Maybe some-day, five or ten years down the road, but I can't handle it right now. I don't know how to be a good mother, and I'd rather not be one at all if I can't be a good one. I know Ginger will be fine with you. You're so great with her. You're a terrific dad and a terrific guy, Ben. You deserve a lot better than me. I'm so sorry we didn't wait until we were older. There's still so much I want to do first. Please try to understand.

Tina

I took my time refolding the letter. I felt a little bad for Ginger. If I hadn't suggested the idea of finding her mama, she probably wouldn't have gone snooping through her daddy's stuff. But I felt a lot worse for myself. Suddenly Operation Finding Tina didn't seem so simple.

"See," Ginger said. "She didn't love me."

"It doesn't say that. It just says she wasn't ready to be a mama yet."

"Same thing."

"No, it isn't. Not at all. She wanted to be a good mama. She just didn't know how yet."

"She thought I was a pain. She didn't want to be stuck at home with me."

"How old was she, again?"

"Nineteen."

"Well, that is kind of young."

"Yeah, well, Daddy was young, too. If he could do it, how come she couldn't?"

"I don't know. Maybe it depends on the person."

"What I don't get is why she had to be stuck at home every day. Why didn't she just go and do what she wanted and take me with her like other mamas do?" Before I could come up with any kind of answer, she sat up and grabbed the letter from my hand. "Yeah, well, I'm not trying to find her."

"But it says she'd be ready further down the road. That probably means she's ready now."

A knock sounded on the door. Ginger crammed the letter and envelope under her pillow.

Ben opened the door and stepped in, and the room seemed to shrink. It was a perfect rerun of the evening when he and Mama had caught us looking at the phone book, only this time he wasn't smiling. My heart started jumping like peas on a hot griddle.

"What's goin' on here? Why are you crying, Ginger?"

"I'm not. Everything's fine, Daddy."

I focused on all the tiny green flecks of grass clinging to Ben's shoes.

"You girls been fighting again?"

"No, sir," we said together.

"Well, come on outside. I have a job for you two."

Ginger and I rolled our eyes at each other as we followed him. What would he think if he knew what was hiding underneath her pillow?

He led us around the side of the house to a wide patch of dug-up earth in the backyard. Eight oily railroad ties lay piled beside it.

"Here's where your mama's garden's gonna be," he said.

I blinked. Mama always talked about wanting a garden. "Does she know yet?"

"Nope. Just brought in the ties last night. I want to have it done by the time she gets off work tonight so we can surprise her." It was nice of him to say "we" instead of "I."

"Anyhow," Ben said, "there's a million and one pecans that need to be picked up before I can mix in the manure. You kids can work for an hour before the sun makes its way around here."

Ginger groaned.

Ben brought over a wheelbarrow and parked it near us. "Call me when you get it full and I'll dump it. I'll be around front."

Ginger waited until he disappeared around the side of the house, and then she slumped against the wheelbarrow.

I knew she was still sad about her mama, so I worked by myself for a while, sifting through nuts and rocks and trying to think of a way to save Operation Finding Tina. But when the wheelbarrow got half-full and Ginger still hadn't picked up a single nut, I started feeling put-out instead of sorry. "You're s'posed to be helping, you know."

"I don't feel like picking up nuts."

"Yeah, well, go tell your daddy that."

"He's gonna be your daddy soon, too."

I bristled. "No, he's not. I already have a daddy."

"*Had* a daddy, you mean. Just like I had a mama."

I aimed low with my next pecan, and it hit Ginger square in the ribs. She hopped up with a yelp. *"He-e-e-y."*

"Whoops. Sorry."

She rubbed her side. "Sorry, nothing. You did that on purpose."

"Well, jeez, Ginger. You're sitting against the wheelbarrow. What do you expect?"

She scooped up her own pecan and hurled it so fast that all I had time to do was hunch my shoulders, but it whizzed right past. I smirked. "Thought you didn't feel like picking up nuts."

"I don't. But I feel like throwing them at you."

We eyed each other silently. Ginger's eyes were almond—so light they almost didn't have a color.

"No throwing at the head," I said.

She kicked a pile of dust at me. I closed my eyes to shield them as the air filled with flying pecans. My shin burned as if it'd been shot, followed by my belly a second later. I hopped around on one foot, trying to rub my leg and throw at the same time. I got her in the ribs twice before she ducked down behind the wheelbarrow.

"Get out from there," I yelled. "I don't have nothing to hide behind."

She pelted me a few times before I scooped up a whole

handful of dirt and nuts and ran around behind the wheelbarrow. She popped up like a jackrabbit and took off.

I gave chase around the yard until I tripped over a railroad tie and landed with a heavy *oomph* right on my stomach. Ginger hurled two pecans at my butt while I tried to catch my breath. I yelped and rolled back to my feet in a hellfire hurry. "You're gonna be dead as a doornail, Ginger!"

She squealed and started running in crazy circles, her big feet kicking up enough dirt to choke a mule. The air turned so thick and brown, I could barely see where to aim. My breath rasped in my chest and I stung all over. I finally reached out my leg and tripped her. Before she could get up, I jumped on her back and twisted her arm up behind her. "Say 'uncle.'"

"Oww!"

"Say it. Say it now."

"I'm gonna kill you, Piper."

"That'll be tough with a broken arm."

She kept struggling, and I didn't think I'd be able to hold on much longer. But I had the advantage of being on top, and finally she said, "Okay, fine. Uncle, you idiot."

I rolled off her and collapsed. We lay next to each other, panting for a little while. Then she turned her head and glared at me through a mask of grime. I grinned. "You look like a raccoon," I said.

"Yeah? You should talk."

I rubbed my shoulder. "You threw pretty good."

"Yeah?" She sounded surprised. "So did you."

"You shouldn't have kept hitting me after I fell."

"Sorry."

"Boy, I could drink a river."

She sat up. "There's Popsicles in the freezer. Want one?"

"Sure," I said.

"Cherry or grape?" We struggled to our feet. Before I could decide, something caught my eye. I turned and saw Ben leaning up against the side of the house, his arms crossed, looking for all the world as though he wanted to come over and whip us both.

"Oh, shoot," Ginger muttered. "How long have you been standing there, Daddy?"

"Long enough."

His voice didn't match the look on his face. He sounded a little like he wanted to laugh. "So, Piper Lee? You figured out how you're gonna explain to your mama why you're covered with bruises tomorrow?"

Ginger snickered.

My eyes were scratchy from grit, and all I wanted to do was wash my face. "I don't know." I bent down and brushed some of the dirt from my bare legs.

Ben chuckled. "Guys throw punches and girls throw nuts, is that it? You two work out whatever you were fussin' about?"

Ginger and I looked at each other. "Yes, sir," we answered together.

"Good," he said. "Now maybe you can get some work done."

8

Ginger and I finished our Popsicles and then filled the wheelbarrow twice before an old farm truck pulled up with a load of black, crumbly cow poop.

"That's gross," Ginger said. "I'm not touching it."

The sun grew hot as blue blazes, but Ben kept on working, heaving railroad ties into place, his T-shirt sticking to him like syrup to a flapjack.

About the time the farm truck left, Ginger whined about having a rock in her shoe and limped off toward the giant oak. She leaned up against the tree, barefoot, picking at one of her toenails. "What did you do?" I asked. "Chip some polish?"

She wrinkled up her nose at me.

Ben smiled.

I guess it was that smile that made me ask, "You want me to spread some of this manure around?"

He raised his eyebrows. "Sure. Rake's over there."

Ginger lazed around in the shade and watched us till Ben sent her inside to make a pitcher of sweet tea. I kept raking, smoothing the dirt, still thinking about the pecan fight with Ginger. Something was different between us, and I wasn't sure I liked it.

By the time Ol' Faithful roared up that evening, Ben had all the railroad ties in place and I had the soil raked smooth. Ginger and I used the garden hose to rinse off the worst of our dirt while Ben went around front to get Mama.

I heard the car door slam and Mama giggle.

"Here she comes," Ginger whispered.

Mama shuffled into view, one of Ben's big hands clamped over her eyes as he guided her toward us. "What in the world's goin' on, Ben Hutchings? And what'd you do with the girls?"

"Sold 'em to a slave trader passing on through. Got a hundred bucks a head." He brought her to a stop right in front of the garden and lowered his hand, nodding to Ginger and me.

"Surprise!" we shouted.

For a split second, confusion flickered across Mama's face, but then she saw what she was supposed to be looking at, and her hand flew to her mouth. "Get out of town. It's a raised bed."

"For your garden," Ben said.

Mama turned and threw her arms around him as though she didn't even notice how dirty and sweaty he was. "Have I ever told you what a great guy you are?"

He hugged her back and winked at me over her shoulder. "I can't take all the credit. The girls helped, too."

Mama gave Ginger and me each a hug, then started gushing about black-eyed peas and beans and collard greens, telling us what-all she was going to plant where.

Right about then is when my stomach started rumbling. "All this talk about food is sure making me hungry."

"Me too," Ginger said.

Mama dug out a pizza from Ben's freezer and put it in to bake while the three of us got a more thorough washup. Ginger loaned me a clean shirt. Then, not long after we'd eaten, Mama pushed her chair back with an unhappy look and said that we'd better get going.

Ben scowled. "Do what? All my hard work today, and all I get is a lousy hour of your time?"

Mama edged over and sat on his knee. "I know. I'm sorry. But I have to get to the bank before it closes, and I told Piper Lee I'd take her to the library for a bit, too. I'll make it up to you, promise."

I tried hard not to act surprised when she mentioned the library; I'd forgotten all about it. Now that Ginger had found the letter, there didn't seem much point in going, but I waited to tell Mama until we were on our way home.

"How come?" she asked. "You seemed so sure about it this morning."

"I just don't feel like going now. Too tired, I guess."

"That garden was sure a surprise. Thank you for helping." She sighed. "Ben's so good about doing nice things for me. He spoils me rotten."

"I bet Daddy did plenty of nice things for you, too."

"Hmm? Oh, well, sure, honey. Course he did."

"Like what?"

She hesitated, as if she might answer wrong and upset me. "Well, he took me out to supper a lot. And he used to buy me flowers—carnations. Those were his favorite. And we'd go dancing sometimes."

"I didn't think you liked to dance."

"I don't, actually. I'm lousy at it. But your daddy loved

it. He just loved going out and doing something, anything—the wild and crazier the better. He was always dragging me here and there." Her voice softened. "I have no idea what drew us together; we were so different."

"What do you mean?"

"Mmm. Your daddy was such a free spirit. He liked to make his own rules, and he loved taking risks." She paused. "He was still in the Air Force at the time, the most exciting man I'd ever met in my life. Plus, the fact that I was only eighteen and he was thirty made him pretty impressive, too."

"Sounds like a lot of fun."

"Oh, you bet. We had tons of fun. But then you came along and the risk-taking didn't seem so fun anymore. It scared me then. Funny how having a baby changes your whole outlook on things."

I studied my hands. Even though I'd scrubbed them hard, black streaks still outlined my fingernails. "You were nineteen when I was born?"

"Almost twenty."

"Were you ready for me?"

"You mean, was I ready to be a mother?"

I nodded.

Mama considered it. "I've never regretted having you,

Piper Lee. But if I could do it over, I think I might have waited a couple years longer. Having babies is a huge responsibility. You really need to wait until you're grown up and ready."

"Ginger's mama wasn't ready," I said.

Mama's shoulders jumped back. "No. No, she wasn't. Some women never are."

"Never?"

"Not everybody wants children, Piper Lee. And that's perfectly okay. Course, the time to decide that is before you have one, not after. But Ben's done a terrific job with Ginger all on his own. That's one of the things that makes me respect him so much."

"But he's not like Daddy, is he? He's not a risk taker."

"Lordy no, thank goodness. I need some stability in my life. But he . . . he's the kind of person who I know will always be there for me. For us. I feel real safe when he's around." She cracked a silly grin. "That and the fact that he's as cute as a speckled pup."

I groaned.

Mama laughed. "And speaking of the raised bed and nice surprises, did Ben happen to mention the surprise he has for you?"

All my muscles tightened. "What surprise?"

"He's scheduled to work the Saturday of the air show, but he signed up to take the afternoon off so the four of us can go together."

It felt as if the car seat dropped away from underneath me.

"That's right," she said. "He's taking four hours of his vacation time to do something you want to do."

"But I never asked him about it."

"I know. I decided to. He already knew about it—said you'd mentioned it the other day at the beach. But I didn't ask him to take time off from work. He came up with that all by his lonesome."

"Wow," I whispered. "I don't believe it."

"Yeah," Mama said. "Pretty nice guy, huh? And what's he gonna get in return?"

It took a while before it dawned on me that she expected an answer. "Oh, um—a thank-you?"

"That'd be a good start, along with a good attitude, maybe. Think you can manage?"

"Yes, ma'am."

Mama reached over and patted my knee. "I'm bushed, too. Let's run by the bank quick and then just go home and watch a movie and kick back. How's that sound?"

"Sure," I said. But I didn't know what I'd just agreed

to. My head buzzed like a honeybee in a whole field of blooms.

That night I snuggled in bed with Mowgli and tried to sort stuff out. I'd been stupid as a loony bird to help Ben with the garden the way I had. I'd been too nice and spent too much time with him. He probably thought I was starting to like him, starting to be okay with him and Mama getting married. Maybe he was trying to make me like him by doing nice things.

That's why he hadn't tattled on me for swimming out to the island. And why he'd offered me money for ice cream. Now he was fixing to take me to the air show. He probably had a plan of his own. A plan called Operation Winning Over Piper Lee.

Maybe going to the air show would be a mistake. But I wanted to go real bad. I already had three dollars saved toward a ride on the sonic boom flight simulator. And I wanted to see the Blue Angels perform their famous Diamond Formation. See the rolls and dives and hear the booms of thunder, maybe even get an autograph from one of the pilots. Just thinking about it made my heart beat faster.

I had to go—but I didn't have to be nice to Ben. I'd say

thank you if Mama remembered to make me, but other than that, I'd pretend he wasn't there at all.

In the meantime, I had to find a way to convince Ginger to give Operation Finding Tina another try. Surely Tina was ready to be a mama by now.

At least I hoped so. I was almost outta time.

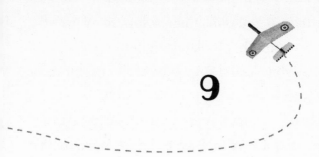

9

"Miss Claudia?" I asked as soon as Mama left for work the next afternoon. "I watered all those flowers out back. Need anything else?"

"You 'member those magnolia shrubs as well?"

"Yes, ma'am."

She glanced up from her sewing machine. "Well, then, no, child, I can't think of nothing else right now."

"Okay, then I think I'll ride my bike to the library for a bit. That all right?"

"I s'pose it is. You asked your mama first?"

"Oh, she won't mind. It's not very far. I'll be back in an hour or so."

She held up two squares of fabric with red roosters on them. "What do you think of these potholders I'm making for your mama? You think these colors are okay?"

"Oh, yes, ma'am. They look just right to me."

"Well, bless your heart. You be careful crossing those streets, now, you hear?"

"I will," I said. "Don't fret about me." Then I scooted out of there real quick, before she had time to realize that I'd never admitted to asking Mama about the library. But once I pedaled out of sight of the apartment, I slowed to give myself time to think.

I didn't like sneaking around behind Mama's back like this. It made my belly feel all antsy. But the wedding raced toward me, and I owed it to Daddy to at least try to do right by him.

I waved to Reverend Thomas as I passed the old Baptist church on the corner of Third and then waited for a delivery truck to pull out of the parking lot of the Taco Cabana on Fifth. By the time I reached the library, I'd talked myself out of feeling quite so nervous. After all, I was trying to bring Ginger and her mama back together. That wasn't anything to feel bad about—it was downright admirable.

I leaned my bike against one of the pillars by the front door and headed inside. I fished my library card out of my pocket as I neared the front desk. "Could I use the Internet, please?"

The library lady didn't look very old, but her glasses dangled from a gold chain around her neck. I thought only old people wore their glasses like a necklace.

"I'll need to see your card, please." She ran it through a scanner and peered at the computer screen. I fidgeted. Maybe the card would somehow tell her what I was up to, that she shouldn't let me use the Internet. But after a minute she smiled and said, "All right, we'll put you on number nine. You can have thirty minutes, and more if you need it as long as no one else is waiting." She scribbled the time on a sheet of paper and slid it across to me. "Need help with anything?"

"No, ma'am. We use the Internet at school all the time." But then I hesitated. "Do you know how to go about finding people?"

"Finding people? You mean like a person's address?"

"Somethin' like that."

"Well, the easiest way would probably be with the online phone book."

I guess she could tell by the look on my face that I didn't have much idea what she meant. She wiggled a finger at me. "Come on, I'll show you."

She led me over to a computer and rolled out the chair. Her long fingers tapped in some letters on the keyboard. She wore pearly pink fingernail polish that made me think of Ginger. The screen flashed to Yahoo and then to the phone book. "Okay. Here you go," she said, pointing. "Type the person's name in this box right here, and any other information you might know in these boxes over here, and then click Enter. That'll get you started."

"Okay. Thanks a lot." I smiled and waited till she walked away, and then I took a quick peek over each shoulder. A couple of little kids sprawled on beanbags in the story-time corner, and a handful of people milled around the magazine racks, but Tuesday afternoon was a quiet time to come to the library. I took a deep breath and searched the keyboard for the letters in Tina's name.

The screen went white for a minute, and then six Tina Lymans flashed up. I couldn't believe it. Two from California, one from Texas, two from Kansas. But one entry made my heart do a somersault. Littleton, Colorado. I took another peek over each shoulder. A fat lady in a flowered tent dress stepped around the end of a row and started toward me, but then she turned down another row and disappeared.

I stared at Tina's name for a long time. Now what? I hadn't expected it to be so easy. I jotted down the Colorado phone number and started to close the page. That's when I noticed the pop-up ad. *"Need to find someone? We can help—Real Investigations for Real Answers."*

Maybe it would be another way to find out more about Tina.

"Are you searching for a lost loved one? Let us help. There's a good chance some of our forum members may be able to answer your questions or provide valuable information. Share your thoughts and stories here, and get the help and support you need. Registration is free."

A tingle started at my neck and zipped clear down to my toes. It seemed as if those words were just for me. How come I'd never thought about doing any kind of search like this for Daddy? I read over some of the subject topics posted. There was a daddy looking for his two daughters. A college student trying to find her missing roommate. A mama looking for her eight-year-old son.

There were twelve topics to a page and at least ten pages. "Boy, howdy," I whispered. I'd never guessed how many lost persons there might really be. And how many people might be looking for them. Could someone out there know about Daddy? Maybe somebody knew if he was still alive or even where he might be.

I glanced at the little slip of paper from the library lady. Fifteen minutes left. It didn't take long to register and pick a username, but then I had to figure out how to tell Daddy's story. It was a mighty big story to fit into a small square box.

I'm looking for my daddy. His name is Christopher David DeLuna. He crashed his plane off the Georgia coast four years ago and was never found. I think he's still alive someplace. Maybe he got hurt real bad and has been in a hospital. Or maybe he just can't remember anything. But I would do just about anything to find out. If you think you might know about my daddy or the accident, please let me know.

I thought about adding more, but my time was up. I scribbled the website information on a scrap of paper and clicked back to the library's homepage. Then I darted over to the kids' area and snatched a couple of books so I'd have something to show if Miss Claudia asked what I'd done at the library.

I raced home as fast as I could pedal, feeling so full of

myself that I could've lifted right off the seat and flown. Not only did I find Tina, I might've found out something about Daddy, too.

I checked in with Miss Claudia and took a minute to ooh and aah over her progress on the potholders before slipping back across the hall. I hovered at the kitchen table, studying Tina's phone number for a good ten minutes. Finally I found the courage to pick up the phone.

I punched in a 1 and then the ten-digit number, clutching the phone real tight.

One ring.

Two rings.

Maybe nobody was home.

Three rings.

Four rings.

What if an answering machine came on?

"Hello?" The lady's voice paralyzed me.

"Hello?" she repeated.

"Uh, yes, ma'am, hello," I got breath enough to say. "I—I'm looking for Tina. Tina Lyman."

"This is Tina."

"Are you the Tina that used to live in Georgia?"

"At one time I did. Who is this?"

"My name's Piper Lee. I think you and my mama went to school together." The lie slid off my tongue as slick as melted butter off a cob of sweet corn.

"Oh, really? Who's your mom?"

"Her name's Heather. Heather DeLuna."

"I don't recognize the name. Are you sure you have the right Tina?"

My mouth turned as dry as sunbaked clay. "This isn't some sort of joke, is it?" she asked. "Because I was just on my way out and I don't have time to fool around."

"Are you Ginger's mama?" I blurted.

Silence.

It went on so long, I feared maybe she had hung up on me. But then she said, "How do you know Ginger?"

I almost hung up myself. If I answered that question, there was no turning back. "Her daddy's gonna marry my mama."

The lady made a strange little whistling noise under her breath. "Ben's getting remarried?"

"Yes, ma'am."

"When?"

"September tenth."

"Oh . . . wow. What's your mama's name, again?"

"Heather DeLuna."

"Tell me about her. I bet she's pretty."

I didn't know what to say. Why ask about Mama? She was supposed to ask about Ginger. "Well, yeah, she's pretty . . . um, and she's a waitress."

"How long has she been dating Ben?"

"About a year now."

"Does he still work at the prison?"

"Yes, ma'am."

"Why did you call me, Piper Lee?"

I swallowed. "I found your number. I—I did it for Ginger. She talks about you sometimes."

"Yeah? What's she say?"

"I think she just wonders about you, is all. How you are." *And why you walked out on her,* I almost added.

"Well, she's got a great father. She doesn't need me. I'm afraid to say I've never been too much of a kid person."

I replayed those words over in my head, listening real hard, sure I'd missed something—something to show she was sorry about the way things had worked out. But there was nothing.

"She wants to be a cheerleader," I said.

Tina laughed. "Oh, well, she must have a bit of me in her. I was on the drill team."

"I guess she must."

"Well, if there's nothing more you need, I better go. You tell Ginger hi and that I'm doing fine and that I hope she is, too. All right?"

"All right," I said. She hung up before I could say good-bye. I sat there, full of shivers, trying to puzzle out why the conversation had gone so differently than I'd figured it would. Tina was supposed to have been all excited that Ginger was thinking about her. She was supposed to ask what grade Ginger was in, about her favorite class, what kinds of things she liked to do. Maybe how tall she'd gotten, or what she looked like now—the things any mama would want to know.

I balled up the paper with Tina's number and hurled it into the living room. Then I went and flopped down beside the patch of sun where Mowgli lay. His sleepy eyes widened with alarm.

"Yeah," I whispered. "I know how you feel."

I'd found Tina, but how was I supposed to get her back into Ginger's life when she acted as if she didn't care? And if she didn't care, how on earth was I supposed to get her back together with Ben?

Mowgli fixed me with a furious look.

"Don't worry your flat face," I said. "I'm the one with the problem."

I reached out and grabbed the ball of paper, smoothing the worst of the wrinkles. Something told me to hang on to it a bit longer. I took it into my bedroom and opened the cover of my aviation scrapbook. Daddy grinned out at me. I placed the paper on the lower half of the page, where it wouldn't cover his face. "Keep this safe for me," I said. "I just might need it again."

10

MAMA AND I headed to Ben's for supper that evening. My rumbling belly did a pretty good job of pushing the day's events to the back of my mind. It's tough to think on an empty belly.

Ben sizzled pork patties on the barbecue, and the smell made me crazy hungry. I guess it drove the hornets crazy, too, on account of how they grouped overhead. Ginger and I crunched on pork rinds until Mama handed each of us a wedge of watermelon instead.

One of the hornets landed on Ginger's watermelon right as she raised it to her mouth. "Watch out," I said, and slapped at her hands. She squealed like a stuck pig and dropped her watermelon in the dirt.

She stared down at it. "I almost got stung right in the mouth."

I pictured Ginger with her head puffed up like a balloon — a balloon with a French braid. "Probably would've swelled your tongue so bad you couldn't talk. That would've been something."

Ginger didn't act bothered by the teasing. She was busy keeping count of the hornets on her melon. "Three of them now."

"The meat's about done," Ben said a moment later. "Y'all can go in and get your buns ready."

Mama led the way inside. She sliced some Vidalia onions and opened up a big can of pork and beans. I looked at all the beans floating around in the brown-sugar sauce and wondered why they bothered to put the word *pork* on the label. They were just beans with a tiny piece of fat. They sure did taste good, though. Ginger and I pulled out the mayonnaise and pepper sauce and an icy cold six-pack of root beer from the fridge.

Ben brought in a platter of steaming meat, waving the hornets away as he came through the door. We'd just started passing food around the table when the phone rang.

"Don't answer it, Daddy," Ginger said. "Just say the blessing. I'm starved."

Ben hesitated, then shrugged and said, "Aw, just let the machine get it." He said a quick blessing over the ringing.

I took my first bite, and the wonderful salty taste of smoked pork filled my mouth.

"Hello there, Ben," said a lady's voice on the machine. I nearly choked. I knew that voice. It was Tina.

I could tell Ben knew, too. He froze, the bottle of pepper sauce tilted in his hand.

"I hear you're getting married," she continued. "I just wanted to say congratulations and maybe talk to Ginger a bit. Sometimes I miss that little girl an awful lot, you know. I'll give a call back tomorrow night and see if you're around then."

Ginger looked as though somebody had sneaked up and walloped her from behind. "That was Mama. That was her, wasn't it, Daddy?"

Ben lowered the bottle of pepper sauce.

"I believe . . . so," Mama answered for him.

"How in the world would she know about the wedding?" Ben said. "We haven't spoken a word in ages."

I got a real strong urge to go pee. I buried my face in a big bite of pork patty.

Ginger dashed over to the answering machine and replayed the message. "She's gonna call again tomorrow. Can I talk to her?"

Ben grimaced as though he'd been stung by a hornet. "In a pig's eye."

Ginger's face turned into a huge wrinkle. "What? Why not? She misses me, didn't you hear? She wants to talk to me!" Her voice went up, up, up, with each word till she was nearly hollering by the last one.

Ben shoved his chair back. "Scuse me a minute." The screen door creaked open and slammed behind him. The whoosh of air sent a ball of plastic wrap rolling across the table.

Ginger crept back over and peered into Mama's face. "Why doesn't he want me to talk to her, Heather? I need to. I've never got to before."

Mama's eyes darted from Ginger to me to the screen door. I could tell she didn't have a clue what to say. "I think he's just a little put-out right now, honey. Give him a minute."

My insides felt as shook up as a bottle of salad dressing. I couldn't believe Tina had actually called. *Sometimes I miss that little girl an awful lot.* Why did she pretend to miss Ginger when she hadn't even asked me about her? *I'll give a call back tomorrow night.* Would she? And if she did call, would she tell Ben how she'd learned of the wedding? How in the world would I explain myself? And how come I'd been so dumb as not to see this problem ahead of time?

Ginger slipped back into her chair. I picked at the rest of my food, but there wasn't much left of my appetite. After a while, Mama lifted her glass of sweet tea and stood. "I think I'll go check on your daddy now."

"Tell him I need to talk to her," Ginger whispered. "Please?"

The screen door creaked open again, and Mama let it close gently behind her.

Ginger kneeled in her chair to peek out the kitchen window.

"Can you see them?" I asked.

"They're on the porch swing." She ducked back down. "I didn't think she'd ever call again. Maybe she does care about me, just a little, no matter what that letter said."

"Course she does," I said, thankful that Ginger seemed too distracted to connect me to the phone call.

I started stacking plates, and Ginger put the refrigerator stuff away. We left Ben's plate of food on the table. He hadn't taken a single bite. His and Mama's voices were a low murmur outside, barely loud enough for us to tell which of them was talking. But all of a sudden they got louder, and then louder still, until Ben sounded plain riled up and Mama barely spoke at all. It was the closest they'd ever come to arguing, and knowing it was my fault didn't feel good.

Ben strode through the door a moment later. Ginger and I scooted out of his way as he sat down at the table and took his first bite.

Mama wandered in behind him looking a little teary-eyed. She forced a smile and pushed a strand of hair back from her face. "Come on, Piper Lee. I think we best go home."

Ben shook his head. "I never said I wanted you to leave, Heather."

"I know. I just think the two of you need a little time to talk. You can give me a call later if you like."

"This is not the way supper was s'posed to go."

Mama patted his shoulder. "I know, guy. But it was a real good supper anyhow, wasn't it, Piper Lee?"

I nodded. "Especially the pork."

Ginger hovered by the sink, not saying a word, but I could tell she didn't want us to go. I tried to think of something nice to say, but my brain was doing too much bouncing around. "See ya later," I said.

I waited until we turned off Hillman Lane and onto the main road before asking, "Why doesn't Ben want Ginger to talk to her mama?"

"'Cause, honey. He's worried she might get hurt."

"Does he think Tina's a bad person?"

"No, not a bad person, just . . . irresponsible, you might say. And he's not real sure what Tina's motive is. He doesn't feel he can trust her."

"I still don't get it, Mama. How can Ginger get hurt just by talking to her?"

Mama didn't answer right away. She drummed her thumbs on the steering wheel. "You know how sometimes when you only know bits and pieces about somebody, you're forced to let your imagination fill in all the rest? And when it's a person you really wish you knew, you tend to put them up real high on a pedestal, so high they can start to seem almost perfect . . . kind of like you do with your daddy."

"I know Daddy wasn't perfect."

"But when you think of him, you only recollect good things, right? Like how he was funny, and brave, and a respected pilot. You probably don't recall how impatient he got with slow drivers, or how he spanked your behind the time you threw your cup of milk off the table, or how he got cranky if I talked too long on the phone. I bet you don't recollect any of those things."

I wanted to tell her she was wrong, that I remembered lots about Daddy—good and bad. But I couldn't. I felt as though she'd sucker-punched me.

Mama sighed. "Your daddy was all the good things you remember, Piper Lee. But he was also a flesh-and-blood person with quirks and flaws like the rest of us. And so is Tina. In fact, if you look at her track record, she's a downright selfish person. And Ben's afraid Ginger thinks she's near perfect, and that if she talks to her mama and finds out she's not, she might be real disappointed."

I nodded to show Mama I understood, but I knew Ginger didn't think Tina was perfect. Especially not after finding that letter in her daddy's box. "So is he not gonna let the two of them talk?"

"I convinced him he ought to."

"Is that what you were fighting about?"

"We weren't fighting, Piper Lee. I was just trying to help him see that if he doesn't allow Ginger to talk to her mama, she'll surely resent him for it."

Mama smiled as if everything were just fine, but once we got home, she paced from one part of the house to another. She puttered around in the bathroom for a bit, then gazed out the kitchen window for a while, then finally sat down to fix a hole in one of the aprons she wore at work.

I spread some newspaper on the kitchen table and brought out my model ARV Super2. If I could get the wheels assembled, I'd finally be to the painting stage. But some of the parts were so tiny, they were almost impossible to work with. I used Mama's tweezers to lift a tire and dropped on a single drip of glue, but when I tried to fix it in place, it slipped free and landed on the newspaper. I grabbed it up quick before it could stick and tried again — and again. I wished I'd stuck with the level 3 models instead of convincing Mama I was ready for a level 4.

"I'm thinking now that maybe we shouldn't have left," Mama announced out of the blue.

"Why's that?"

"I just feel funny about walking out, leaving Ginger like I did. I think she needed me to stay."

"She's got Ben there."

"I know. There's just times when a girl needs a mama around."

Hot pressure flowed down from the top of my head. "You talk like you're her real one."

Her sharp look shamed me. "No, Piper Lee, I'm not her mother from birth. But in this past year alone I've been more of a mama to her than Tina ever has. Most any woman can carry a baby inside her, but it's the one who loves you and tries to raise you up right that makes a real parent. You remember that."

I tried to swallow, but my throat felt all closed up, as if it were full of model glue.

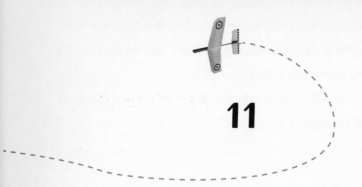

11

THE NEXT MORNING after breakfast Miss Claudia called me over and asked if I'd like to earn a few dollars. She led me into her bedroom and pointed to a huge plastic flowerpot full to the brim with pennies.

"Wow, Miss Claudia, how long have you been saving these?"

"A long while now. I've no idea how many there are, but if you roll them for me, I'll give you twenty percent of the total."

I stared at the pot and mulled things over for a minute. Rolling that many pennies would take forever and a day, but then I remembered the sonic boom simulator ride at the air show. I had three dollars saved up—surely there were enough pennies to earn me the other four dollars I needed. "Yes, ma'am," I said. "I'll do it."

Miss Claudia clapped her hands like a little kid getting a present and said, "Well, bless your heart." She lifted the edge of the quilt hanging over her bed. "There's a whole sack of penny rolls under the bed here. Do you mind savin' my old knees and getting them for me?"

I groped around in the dark until I found the paper bag. It was so coated with dust that it made me sneeze. I dumped a bunch of penny rolls out onto the carpet and pushed the bag back under the bed.

"Jus' holler if you need me," Miss Claudia said. "I got some kitchen towels I'm making for your mama, to go along with the potholders. They're just the cutest things—red and green like a watermelon."

Her saying "watermelon" made me think about Ginger dropping her wedge on account of the hornets. I wished I could go just one single day without thinking about her, or Ben, or the wedding. I stacked pennies into little towers of ten and fretted over Operation Finding Tina. I didn't know what the next step should be, or if there even *was* a next step.

I'd piled thirty-four penny rolls into a pyramid when

Mama stopped by to tell me she was headed to work. She paused out in the living room to talk with Miss Claudia, and after a bit I noticed she'd dropped her voice down low. I crawled over to the doorway.

" . . . after four years, just out of the blue," Mama said.

"Well, I'll be hog-wallered," Miss Claudia said. "What could she be thinking?"

"Maybe it's some sort of control issue. She wouldn't tell Ben how she knew about the wedding. Just said she knew more about things than he thought."

I went limp as a dishrag with relief. Ben had talked with Tina and she hadn't tattled on me. Maybe she wouldn't. Maybe she liked making Ben puzzle over the mystery.

"I surely wouldn't worry too much over it," Miss Claudia said. "I just don't see how that girl would have a leg to stand on after walking out the way she did."

"You wouldn't think," Mama said. "But I'm afraid she walked out because of Ginger, not Ben. I think she loved him."

"Well, surely she doesn't think she can waltz back in and pick up right where she left off?"

"No, Ben set her pretty straight on that. But she could still cause trouble for us if she wants."

"You know what that girl's problem is, don't you?" Miss Claudia said. "Jealousy. Pure and simple."

"I think so, too. I'm just praying Ginger doesn't get hurt over it."

"Now, that little girl is one hundred percent Ben's, and her mama knows it."

"Maybe," Mama said. "But you know how things work nowadays. She could demand visitation, maybe even sue for custody."

Goose bumps popped up all over my arms. What if Tina tried to take Ginger away from Ben? Never in a million years would I have thought up such a thing.

Miss Claudia heaved a big grumble of a sigh. "Well, it's like the Good Book says, Heather: 'Each day is sufficient for its own badness.' So don't fret too much about what could happen when it likely won't happen at all."

"Course you're right," Mama said, and I could tell she was smiling. "And now I better skedaddle 'fore I make myself late. You know, I do so appreciate all your help with Piper Lee while I'm at work."

"My help? Why, she's the one in there helpin' me right now."

"Bye again, Piper Lee," Mama called.

I skittered back to the middle of the room. "Bye, Mama."

I was all in a flap after that. I kept losing track of my counting and had to start over. I finally stretched out on my back across Miss Claudia's carpet and closed my eyes for a minute to get my head to stop spinning. I'd been so scared to call Tina, not knowing how she might react. Never once had I thought she might get all jealous and riled up.

A shiver passed through me when I recalled the Real Investigations website. Deep down, I didn't really expect much to come of it, but what if I was wrong—again? Right then I started wishing I'd given things a bit more thought before posting Daddy's story for all the world to see.

The soft shuffle of footsteps made me spring up before Miss Claudia could come in and catch me flopped over. She brought me a bologna sandwich and a dish of peach cobbler and praised all my hard work with the pennies. I finished counting a couple hours later with a grand total of eighty-nine penny rolls. I set aside the twenty Miss Claudia told me to keep for myself and stacked the rest back in the flowerpot. I hoped they each had fifty cents, but I wouldn't have staked my life on it.

That evening Mama brought home some leftover chicken and pasta from the Black-eyed Pea. After eating, we headed back over to Ben and Ginger's. I wanted to go about as badly as I wanted a tooth pulled, but I knew there wasn't much point in saying that out loud.

When we pulled into the yard, Ben came through the front door with two bottles of beer and set them on the porch railing. I figured that was a pretty clear sign he and Mama were gonna sit on the porch swing and talk, so I traipsed around to find Ginger in the back. She was bouncing on the trampoline, waving purple and white pompoms over her head and wearing one of those short belly shirts that Ben didn't approve of. She looked as cheerful as a cow in clover.

"Hey, Piper Lee, guess what?"

I kicked off my flip-flops and climbed onto the trampoline. "You got to talk to your mama."

"I did, for a whole half hour." She dropped beside me with so much force, I had to brace my arms to keep from being flipped over. "She's taking classes to be a travel agent, and once she's done, she'll be able to fly places for free."

"I'll be able to fly places for free someday, too," I said. "In my very own plane. So what else you talk about?"

"She just moved into a new apartment not too long ago—a real nice one with a swimming pool and a tennis court."

"How come she left the South? Did you ask her that?"

Ginger shrugged. "Wasn't from here to begin with. Daddy says she grew up in Washington State — must be why she talks funny."

"So did you ask how come she never calls or anything?"

Her smile faded a little. "We didn't talk about that. She said she thinks about me a lot, though, and she's gonna call more often now. In fact, she says she's gonna call again tomorrow night."

"What'd your daddy say about that?"

"He don't like it much. He's probably over there tellin' your mama all about it now."

I glanced over toward the house. "Wanna go listen?"

She shook her head. "Probably get licked if we get caught. Daddy's been all bent out of shape since Mama left the message on the machine." She lowered her voice a notch. "It's almost like he's mad at me."

"Nah. He just don't like your mama callin' out of the blue like she did."

"She has a right to call, to talk to me anytime she wants."

"Mama thinks she's just jealous."

The look on Ginger's face made me want to grab those words and stuff them back into my mouth.

"Say what, Piper?"

"Nothing much. She just thought that, well, your mama calling real sudden-like must have to do with your daddy getting married again."

"That just gave her an excuse to call. She really called 'cause she was thinking 'bout me. You even heard her say it on the machine the other night."

"I know," I said. "It's just that if she misses you so much, why'd she wait till now to come back in the picture?"

"I don't know," Ginger said. "I told you we didn't talk about that. Besides, haven't you ever done something you wish you hadn't? You don't want to talk about it, and you don't want other people to talk about it either, right? So why would I go and make her feel all bad about something she already feels bad about?"

"Okay, okay. Don't go getting all riled up about it."

Her bottom lip trembled. "I'm not. But you don't know what it's like, Piper Lee."

"What what's like?"

"To go your whole life thinking your mama don't care about you, and then to find out that maybe she does after all, but then to still have people telling you that she don't."

I didn't feel much bigger than a June bug right then. "Sorry," I whispered. "I didn't mean it like that."

Ginger barely talked to me the rest of the evening. She said, "Pass me a spoon, please," when we went inside to make root-beer floats, and she said, "Bye," when Mama and I walked out the door. Those six words—that was it. I couldn't really blame her—I didn't feel much like talking to me either.

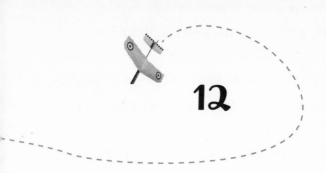

12

MY NEXT CHANCE to sneak away to the library came Thursday after Mama left for work. I waited till Miss Claudia was busy slicing peaches for her next batch of cobbler and then asked if I could go look for a book on model airplanes.

"As long as you promise to hurry on back," she said.

I headed for the library, trying not to get my hopes up so as to save myself the disappointment. But I still couldn't help feeling all tingly when I asked to use a computer. Hundreds, maybe thousands, of people could have seen my post. Surely somebody knew something.

As soon as I logged on to the Real Investigations website, I saw there'd been no reply. The comment box sat empty below my story about Daddy. An ache spread from my throat down to my stomach as I stared at the screen, hoping I'd missed something. But there was nothing.

I was halfway home before I realized I'd forgotten to look for a book on model airplanes, but I didn't care.

I knew it would be better to stay away from the library for at least a few days. But when the chance to go came up again the very next morning, I couldn't resist. Miss Claudia asked if I would ride my bike to Dib's Market for a pint of cream, and said to buy myself a candy bar for the effort.

The offer of the candy bar was good enough, but even better, the market was only two blocks from the library. I ordered myself not to get excited, and I promised myself that if there was no news, I'd let at least three days pass before I checked again.

I must have done a pretty good job of not getting my hopes up, because my heart nearly jumped into my throat when I saw there was a reply to my post. It was from someone with the username of People Hunter. I hunched toward the screen, hoping to block it from anyone who might sneak up behind me.

Hey, Piper Lee —

Nice to meet you. Sorry to hear about your dad. My name is Lyn and I'm from Savannah. I'm a pilot, so I follow all the aviation stories. Your tale rang a bell with me, and I might be able to help you dig up some information. But first I need to know more. How old are you? What town are you from, and what was the date of the accident? Is anyone else helping you search? Let me know and I'll see what I can do.

Lyn

I curled my fingers around the metal frame of the chair to anchor myself in place. If not for all the folks milling around the library, I might've come right up off that seat. I couldn't believe it. Somebody really wanted to help me find out about Daddy. A real pilot—and a lady pilot, at that. And she didn't even live very far away.

I started tapping out answers to Lyn's questions. But it wasn't till after I hit Post that I noticed the alarm ringing in my head, warning me I'd just done something I should've asked Mama about first. She'd let me talk with a stranger on the Internet about as soon as she'd let me jump out my bedroom window. But if I asked her, I'd never get the chance to find out if Lyn knew anything or not. As hard as it was to keep the secret about Tina, now I had another to keep.

I stopped by the market for Miss Claudia's cream and then pedaled home, sucking on a sweet chunk of chocolate. It tasted good, but it would've tasted even better without all the worrisome thoughts swirling through my mind. How long would it take Lyn to answer? What would she say? How long would it be before I could get back to the library to check? Had Tina called Ginger? Would she? What if she tried to cause problems like Mama feared?

I didn't get any of my questions answered until the next night, when Mama and I went over to Ben and Ginger's for supper. As soon as we pulled into the driveway and I saw Ginger hanging around the front porch looking all puny and sad, I knew it probably meant Tina hadn't called. I wasn't sure if that was good or bad.

Mama walked over and put the back of her hand on Ginger's forehead. "Are you feeling sickly, kiddo?" Ginger mustered up a little smile and shook her head. "Yeah? Well, you don't feel feverish. Where's your daddy?"

"Inside. Getting the hamburger patties." Ginger ambled over to the picnic table and dropped down onto the bench.

Mama shot me a look that said *Do something to make her feel better.* Then she headed in to check on Ben.

I stood in the shade of the sunflowers, trying to decide what to do. "You want to jump on the trampoline?" I asked.

"Not now."

"Wanna do something else, then?"

She shook her head. I went and sat down on the bench beside her. Usually she kept her hair pulled back, but today it hung long and loose and blocked most of her face. I wasn't sure when I'd started caring how Ginger felt, but right then I felt puny along with her. I leaned in close and whispered, "Don't feel too bad 'bout your mama. Bet she calls tomorrow."

"Piper Lee," Ben said.

Maybe it was because my nerves were already jumpy or because I didn't know he'd come outside, but when Ben said my name like that, my heart nearly fell out of my chest. "Yes, sir?"

"Whatcha want?"

"N-nothing. I was just talking to Ginger, is all."

Ben raised his eyebrows and waved the barbecue tongs at me. "I was asking what you want — hamburger or hot dog?"

"Oh — uh, a hot dog, please." I glanced back at Ginger.

I couldn't tell if she'd heard what I'd said about her mama or not. She didn't act like it.

We were halfway through a quiet supper when a UPS delivery truck roared into the driveway.

Mama smiled at Ben. "Let me guess. You ordered more parts for that Mustang of yours?"

Ben set his hamburger down. "No, ma'am, not lately I haven't."

He walked over to meet the truck, and the driver placed a medium-size cardboard box into his hands.

Ginger perked up a bit. "Who's it from, Daddy? It's not for me, is it?"

Ben flipped the package to read the address as he headed back to us. His expression turned as dark as if a storm were brewing, and his lips moved with a single, silent word. He set the box onto the picnic table and said, "Yeah, Ginger. It's for you."

Ginger leaned over for a closer look. She squealed. "It's from Mama! She sent me something!"

A look passed between Ben and Mama. The muscles in Ben's jaw began pumping in and out while Ginger hopped around like a crazed chipmunk.

"Open it, Daddy. Do you have your knife?"

Ben reached into the pocket of his jean shorts and fished around. Coins clinked. Then he pulled out his pocketknife and sliced the packing tape real slow and careful, as if he were handling a snake that might bite.

The evening sun beat hot on my bare shoulders as Ginger tore through the crumpled white tissue paper. I shoved a big bite of hot dog into my mouth.

She lifted a hardback book from the box—*The Complete Cheerleading Book of Cheers, Chants, and Jumps*. I felt better as soon as I saw the title; who'd want a dumb gift like that? There was a necklace, too—a silver chain with a little cheerleading megaphone dangling on it. Ginger touched the megaphone like it was something holy, her eyes shining, and then held it up for all of us to see. But it was the last gift that seemed to affect her the most: a little teddy bear wearing a blue and white T-shirt with the words *Somebody in Colorado Loves Me*. None of us said a word, not even Ginger. She just held the little bear against her chest and closed her eyes for a bit.

I took another bite of hot dog as she pawed through the box, making sure she hadn't missed anything. Then her eyes got wide and she said, "Hey, Piper Lee." She held out a wrapped package with my name printed across the paper.

I struggled to swallow. Tina had actually sent me something? I couldn't believe it. I wanted to grab that package and rip it right open, but Mama was making that little sound in the back of her throat—the one she made when she was a hair away from getting riled up.

"I'll open it for you," Ginger said.

No way was I letting that happen. I snatched it from her and yanked off the single strip of tape before Mama could tell me not to.

"It's a plane," Ginger said. "You ought to like that."

"It's not just a plane." My excitement bubbled up. "It's an X-stream Future Glider, like they advertise on TV." I ran my fingers over the glider's black and white foam body and yellow wings. "These things are s'posed to fly sixty yards."

Mama forced a tight little smile. "Ben," was all she said.

He sighed and rubbed the back of his neck. "All right," he said. "I'm done, done."

Ginger put a protective arm around her gifts.

I clutched my glider.

Ben covered the distance between the picnic table and the porch in three long strides.

Mama darted after him. "Wait, guy. Don't call when you're angry. We have to be careful how we handle this."

"Daddy?" Ginger called after him. "If you're gonna call Mama, can I talk to her? Just to say thank you?"

Ben pointed a finger at her right before he and Mama

disappeared through the screen door. "You can stay put, is what you can do." The screen door banged, bounced open, and banged again.

Ben's hamburger sat on his plate. Funny how Tina always managed to interrupt supper.

Ginger sighed—a deep, sad kind of sigh. It made me want to tell her about Tina's phone number. I bit down on the inside of my cheek to keep my mouth shut. Ginger fingered the little megaphone on the necklace and then put the chain around her neck and fooled with the clasp.

"Need some help?" I asked.

She nodded, and I went around behind her and fastened the necklace. Then I took my plane out into the center of the yard, pulled back my arm, and let the glider fly. It sailed way up above the rooftop to the upper branches of the pecan trees, making cool little dips and arcs just like a real plane. It made a final turn and came in for a graceful landing near the porch. I wished I could shrink myself real tiny so I could climb aboard and pilot it. Just thinking about that made me shiver.

"Gee willikers," Ginger said. "That thing really flies. Can I try it?"

"Didn't think you liked planes."

"How would you know? I don't recall us ever talkin' about it."

I couldn't think of a single thing to say to that.

"Sure," I said. "You can try." I trotted over to retrieve the glider and sailed it back toward Ginger. She craned her neck as the plane swooped and looped above her. "How's it make those turns like that?"

"It's all wing design. It's got a real good structure."

She waited for it to land and then scrambled over and scooped it up. "Hold it a little farther back," I said as she got ready to launch it. "Back by the tail."

She repositioned her fingers and let it fly. "Hey, cool. Look at it go."

We played until Ben and Mama came back outside. It didn't seem right to fly the glider in front of them. Ben sat down and finished his hamburger. Mama sipped on a Coke and smiled at me. I was dying to know what had happened inside the house. I could read on Ginger's face that she wanted to know even worse than me, but she didn't ask. She just asked to be excused, packed her gifts back into the box, and headed inside. I followed with the glider.

Ginger propped the teddy bear on her pillow, then flopped across her bed and started thumbing through the cheerleading book. I sat down on the floor, with my back up against the bed, and studied the wing design of the glider. "It sure was nice of your mama to send me this. You must've told her I like planes."

"Told her you were gonna be a pilot and I'm gonna be a professional cheerleader."

"What'd she say about that?"

"Not much. But she must think it's a cool idea or she wouldn't have sent me the book, huh? I wonder what Daddy told her. It makes me so mad he won't let me call on my own. Just don't make sense."

"Where did he get her number?"

"Said he's always had it. He won't tell me where, though. I looked in his address book, but it's not there."

"Maybe he just keeps it in his head."

Ginger sighed. "Maybe it's in the box where I found the letter."

Something in her voice made me shift so I could see if her face was as sad and wishful as her words. It was. She saw me looking at her. "What?"

I stood and peeked out her window. Mama and Ben still sat at the picnic table, but it didn't look as if they were talking. Mama was hunched forward with her chin in her hand. I turned back to Ginger. She was watching me with cat eyes, cautious and curious. "What?" she said again.

My secret was itching to bust free. But could I trust her? Something told me I could, but it was still scary. I dug my fingers into the wood of the windowsill. "Ginger, if I told you a really big secret, would you swear to keep your mouth shut?"

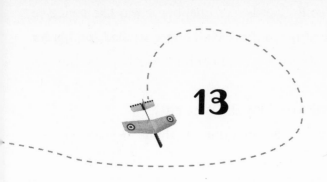

13

GINGER'S JAW DROPPED open wide enough for me to see her tongue. "You have my mama's phone number?"

"Hush," I hissed. "You don't have to let the whole neighborhood know. 'Member how we talked about looking it up on the Internet? Well, I went to the library and did it. Wasn't even hard—her name came right up."

"How . . . I mean, does your mama know?"

"Course not. And you swore to keep your mouth shut, 'member?"

"So where's it at?"

"At home. I'll get it to you soon as I can."

Ginger seemed a little dazed. "Why'd you do it, Piper? Why do you want me to find her so bad?"

Her question hung in the air. I shook my head and waited for some words to come, but it was like trying to pump water from a dry well. Ginger studied me harder with each passing second, her chin tipped up and her lips tight.

"I did it for you," I said. "Why else?"

She snorted. "Never done anything nice for me before."

"Well," I said, "guess there's a first and last time for everything, now, isn't there?"

She seemed to mull things over, keeping her eyes on me as she fingered her necklace. Finally she said, "Piper, what makes you so sure your daddy's still alive?"

I sagged down a little. Didn't she know that hardly a day went by when I didn't ask that same question of myself? Why did I believe? Because Daddy's body never turned up? Or because believing made it easier? "Because," I said softly, "they never found him."

"But it's been four years. If he was alive, he would've —"

"So what? Look how long your mama waited."

"That's 'cause she feels guilty, I think. Your daddy wouldn't have anything to feel bad about."

Her words made me catch my breath. It was true — Daddy didn't have anything to feel bad about. But I couldn't say the same for myself. Tears came sneaking up out of nowhere, flooding my eyes so fast that I didn't have a chance to wipe them away before they spilled over. "Just leave me alone," I said. "You don't know anything about my daddy."

I wanted to run out of the room, but there wasn't really any place to run to, except maybe under the trampoline. But then I'd have to go right past Mama and Ben. I slipped down onto the carpet below the window and kept my head ducked while I wiped hard at my face.

The only sound in the room was my sniffling, then silence.

"I used to have lots of dreams," Ginger suddenly said. "About Mama. Used to be all I thought about when I was little."

"What about her?"

"Mostly about her and Daddy getting back together. I'd picture Mama and me going shopping or swimming or baking cookies, and I'd try to imagine what it would be like to have her around. I used to ask Daddy why he couldn't just go get her and make her come back and be with us."

"What'd he say?"

"Don't recall. Anyhow, then he met Heather and . . ." Ginger paused until I met her eyes. One corner of her mouth lifted in a half smile, as though she was afraid to finish her sentence. "And it's kind of how I pictured it could be, just with a different person."

I swallowed. "Don't it make you feel guilty, though? Like you're not being true?"

"Is that how my daddy makes you feel?"

I heard a woodpecker start drumming outside, and I was thankful for its noise. I twined my fingers around one another and took a deep breath.

"The plane wreck was my fault," I said.

"That's crazy, Piper Lee. Why would you think that?"

"The night before the accident, Daddy promised to take me to the park the next day. But when we woke up, it was real windy. He tried to talk me into going some other time. But I got real upset and started crying. I said we had to go because he'd promised. I just kept bugging him and bugging him till he finally said yes. If we'd stayed home, he would've gotten the phone call earlier."

"What phone call?"

"From his friend John. John's daughter and her boyfriend had gone sailing that morning. But the wind pushed them off course and they got lost. John wanted Daddy to take his plane up and see if he could spot them from the air. Mama came to the park, looking for us, to give him the message. But she couldn't find us 'cause I'd talked Daddy into going for ice cream. By the time we finally got home and Daddy talked to John, the windstorm had gotten a lot worse. He shouldn't have tried to fly. Mama told him so, but John was real scared for his daughter. Turns out the daughter was okay, but if Daddy had been home to get the call earlier, he could've gone looking before the storm got so bad. He probably wouldn't have crashed."

Ginger sniffed. "Might've happened anyway. There's no way to tell for sure."

"Maybe there is," I said. "I think I found somebody who knows."

Ginger bobbed her head. "Say what?"

I hated the way I blurted out stuff when I should've kept my mouth shut. But it was too late now. "When I was lookin' for your mama's phone number, I found a site for missing people. I posted a story about Daddy so that if anybody knows something, they can tell me."

Ginger was quiet for a minute, then shook her head. "Bet nobody knows anything."

I didn't expect her to say that, and the worry that she was right made my eyes fill with tears again. I jumped to my feet. "I don't know," I said. "But one thing's for sure—you breathe a word of this to anybody and I'll rip your mama's phone number up."

"Wait a minute. Where you going?"

"The bathroom. That okay with you?"

I locked the bathroom door behind me, sat down on the edge of the tub, and bawled. I was furious at myself for acting like a baby in front of Ginger and even more furious for telling her about Daddy's plane crash.

I dropped my head onto my arms and recalled that day, the way I'd done so many times before. The park, the wind blowing warm and fierce, Daddy pushing me on the swing. I'd begged him to do underdogs, where he'd push me high enough for him to run underneath the swing. And I remembered eating ice cream, bubble gum flavor. But the clearest memories were of going home and hearing Mama tell him about the lost sailboat. She begged him not to fly, said it was too dangerous. I could still hear her voice when she'd said, "Think about your own daughter."

I'd told Mama once that I thought the accident had been my fault, but she'd said the same thing as Ginger, that it was crazy to think that way. But truth was truth, even if a million people told you otherwise. And the truth was, if I hadn't insisted Daddy take me to the park that day, he might still be with us.

I had to wait till Mama got into the shower the next morning before I could call Ginger and give her Tina's phone number. By Sunday evening Ginger had already left three messages, but Tina hadn't answered any of them. And by the time Mama dropped me off at Ben's on Tuesday, Ginger was so grumpy that she was downright impossible to be around. She made me stand guard while she called Tina's number once again, but she still just got the answering machine. She didn't leave another message.

When Ben came inside for lunch, we made bologna and cheese sandwiches and had some leftover watermelon. Ginger asked if we could watch a movie, but Ben said not until she'd washed up the dishes from the night before.

She stuck her lip out in a pout and crossed her arms as if she were two years old. "There's too many of 'em."

"That's what happens when you don't wash up after each meal like you're s'posed to."

"Why can't we get ourselves a dishwasher like everybody else?"

Ben smiled. "We do have one. She's ten years old and has blond hair."

"That's real funny, Daddy. So funny I forgot to laugh."

Ben was headed back outside, but he stopped when she said that. His smile faded. "I suggest you get up and do what you're told or you're definitely not gonna be laughin'."

Ginger hunched her shoulders and her bottom lip twitched. She had her back turned and couldn't see the look on his face, but I could. I used to think it would've been great to see her get a licking, but I didn't feel that way now. I jumped up. "Come on. If you wash, I'll rinse. It won't take so long that way."

Ginger seemed almost relieved I'd given her an easy out. She stood. "Okay, I guess." Ben went on outside.

"Why are you so put-out with your daddy?" I asked her.

She sniffed. "It's his fault Mama won't call back. I think he told her not to."

"Maybe she's just busy. She's going to school and all, 'member?"

Ginger shook her head hard enough to throw one of her pigtails over her shoulder. "Wasn't too busy to call the other two times."

"Maybe she's out of town for a couple days."

"You can call from anyplace." Ginger stuffed the plug into the sink and turned the water on full blast. "Know what I wish, Piper Lee? I wish she'd never called to begin with."

"You do?"

"Yeah. 'Cause before, I didn't care, and now I do, and it's not right."

She shot a long stream of soap into the dishwater, and

a huge mound of bubbles rose. She waited till it reached the top of the sink and then slapped it hard between both hands. Clusters of bubbles flew everywhere. I wiped a glob from my hair. Ginger laughed, but it sounded closer to crying.

I stood frozen, realizing that the exact thing Mama and Ben had worried about had happened—Ginger had gotten hurt. It made me so hot at Tina. What kind of mama didn't return her own kid's phone calls? I decided right then and there that I was gonna call her myself. Tell her just what I thought about the way she was treating Ginger and what a selfish, sorry excuse for a mama she was.

My chance didn't come until Mama left for work the next afternoon. But I had been thinking about it, keeping my anger on a low boil so I wouldn't chicken out. Mama walked me across the hall to Miss Claudia's before work and kissed me goodbye. I waited till I heard the door close at the bottom of the steps, then told Miss Claudia I'd forgotten something and raced back over to our apartment. My hands shook even worse than the first time I'd punched in Tina's number. I almost melted with relief when the answering machine kicked on. It was so much easier to tell off a machine than a real live grownup.

"Hey, it's Tina," came the familiar voice. "Sorry I'm too busy to chat right now, but if it's important, you can always leave your name and number and I'll get back with you when I can."

If it's important? You bet it was important. I bit my tongue, holding back my words till the beep sounded, and then I let loose. "This is Piper Lee again. Ginger wants to know why you won't call her back. She thinks it's plenty important. I know you're busy and stuff, but it's not right that you got her all excited at first, and sent all the presents, and then nothing after that." I paused for a quick breath and then rushed on. "I'm sorry I called the first time. I shouldn't have done that. I wish I hadn't. And . . . and that's all I wanted to say. Bye, now." I lowered the phone but then jerked it back up again. "Oh, and thank you for the glider. It's a real cool glider." I hung up, feeling pumped and proud and buzzing with as much energy as an electric wire.

Now there was something else I had to take care of. I hurried over to Miss Claudia's to tell her I'd be busy working on my scrapbook for a while and then slipped off to the library. I'd been wanting to go there for days, but I'd been unable to think of the right excuse to tell Mama.

The library lady was the same one who had helped me the first time, the one who wore her glasses like a necklace. "Hello again," she said as she jotted down the number of the assigned computer and my allotted time. "Are you still searching for people?"

She had a soft voice that didn't carry very far, but the question still made me want to shush her. "Oh, not really," I said. "Just doing a little research."

"On anything you need help with?"

"Oh, no, ma'am. Just on birds. Birds of the South." I gave her a little nod and then headed for the computer as fast as I could without running. I tapped my thumb on the table as I waited for the Real Investigations website to load. Had Lyn answered? Did she know anything about Daddy? I had my answer a few seconds later. A new post from People Hunter:

Hey, Piper Lee —
Guess what? I've got some friends who work for the coast guard. After some checking around, I found one who remembers your dad's accident. He told me some things I think you'd be interested in and even gave me a few pictures. They're prints, though, so I can't send them digitally. I live only about forty-five minutes away, so I'd be happy to bring them to you. I can run down Thursday evening if you get this in time. I don't know what you look like, so you'll

have to watch for me. I drive a red Ford Thunderbird.

Call me on my cell if there's a place we can meet.

912-555-0154.

Lyn

I forgot to worry about people looking over my shoulder. I almost forgot I was even at the library. Lyn actually knew one of the rescuers—someone who had real information about Daddy. I closed my eyes and saw his beautiful little Piper Cub, with its shining yellow wings and belly and its flashy black markings. I'd never seen a picture of the plane after the crash. Did I want to?

I wrote down Lyn's cell number and clicked off the site. I didn't know how to feel. That alarm was ringing in my head again, and it wasn't so easy to shut it out this time—but I had to find out about Daddy.

When I got home, I dug Lyn's cell number out of my pocket, and it pulled me over to the phone like a magnet. After the first ring, the call went straight to an automated voice mail.

"This is Piper Lee. I got your message today. I'd really like to meet with you and see the stuff you have about my daddy. I can meet you at the library around four o'clock tomorrow if that's okay. It's on the corner of Seventh and

Jefferson. I really hope you can come . . . I'll watch for your car. Bye, now."

I hadn't a clue what would be going on the next afternoon. I was pretty sure I'd be over at Ben and Ginger's. I'd have to convince Ben to take me to the library. I glanced at Daddy's picture in my scrapbook. Sometimes I wished it were smaller so I could carry it with me. Without looking at it, I had a hard time seeing Daddy's smile or hearing his voice. And I had to work real hard to remember that he'd actually lived with me and Mama, that he wasn't just some made-up dream.

But hearing from Lyn was like being tossed a rope just in time to keep the dream afloat a little longer.

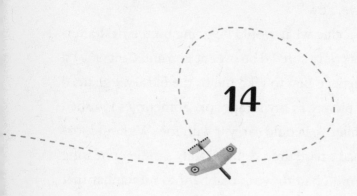

14

I WAITED ON one of the stone benches in front of the library, keeping an eye on the parking lot, though I didn't figure I could miss a red Ford Thunderbird. What a cool car for a pilot to drive. The name made me think of the Blue Angels—loud, fast, powerful.

Ginger sat beside me, dragging her toes through the grass. I wanted her with me about as badly as I wanted a poke in the eye. But Ben had really wanted to stay home and tinker on his Mustang, and I'd needed Ginger's help to come up with the story of overdue books in order to get him to take me to the library. When he agreed to leave us here while he went to buy carburetor fluid, I figured maybe God was on my side after all.

"She'd better hurry up and get here," Ginger said. "Daddy's not gonna be at the auto-parts store much longer."

"Well, if he comes too soon, you gotta distract him for me."

"How am I s'posed to do that?"

"I don't rightly care. Just keep him away. Tell him you found a movie you gotta show him or something."

"What if he asks me who you're talking to?"

I bounced my knees up and down. All Ginger's talk was making me crazy nervous. "I dunno. Just think of something."

"I know," she said, giggling. "I'll just tell him I gotta run in and go pee. It's not like he can come in the girls' bathroom to get me."

I rolled my eyes. "Now, what good would that do? Then he'd just come over to me."

Ginger pulled in a deep breath like she was fixing to reply, but just then a blur of red caught my eye. A Thunderbird turned in off the street. My knees lost their bounce. "Boy, howdy," I whispered. "There she is."

"You sure it's her?"

"How many other people you figure are gonna be in a red Thunderbird?"

I thought maybe I should run over, or at least give a

wave, but I wasn't sure. So I just sat real still as the shiny red car cruised into a parking spot.

The door opened and the driver climbed out. All I saw was a black baseball cap and a bushy black beard to match. I'm not sure if my mouth fell open or not, but I bet it did.

"Uh, Piper Lee," Ginger breathed, "that's a pretty funny-lookin' lady."

The driver shut the door and started toward us. Everything about him seemed long—legs, arms, even his face. He took off his sunglasses and our eyes met. "Hello, there. I'm looking for a Piper DeLuna. One of you girls don't happen to be her, do you?"

"Say no," Ginger ordered.

I swallowed. "Uh . . . yes, sir. I'm Piper Lee. Are you . . . Lyn?"

He smiled. "Let me guess. You were expecting a woman? But Lyn can be a man's name, too, especially if there's only one *n*."

"Oh, see, I—I didn't know that," I stammered. And in those few seconds it dawned on me that I'd never talked with Lyn. Never heard her voice. *His* voice. "Well, thanks for coming down here."

"Glad to help."

"Did you bring the stuff about my daddy? 'Cause I'm afraid I don't have much time."

He gestured over his shoulder. "Sure did. It's right there in the car."

I glanced over at the Thunderbird. "It sure is pretty. Is it new?"

"Fairly new. Would you like to sit in it?"

Before I could answer, Ginger pinched my arm, hard enough to make me glare at her. "What?"

"Sorry," she said out of the side of her mouth, "but Daddy's back already."

I looked over to see Ben's truck ease in just five spaces from the Thunderbird. All my hopes shriveled up like a leaky balloon. If Ben found out I was asking about Daddy—and talking to a stranger—he'd tell Mama for sure.

Lyn studied Ben as he slid out of the truck and started across the lawn toward us. Then Lyn tugged down the bill of his baseball cap and said, "You girls sure picked a fine day to visit the library."

It seemed a funny thing for him to say out of the blue like that. Then he did an even funnier thing—he strolled right on past the stone benches and headed inside. He nodded to Ben as the two of them passed. "Afternoon," he said.

"Afternoon," Ben said, before turning to us. "Come on, you two. Let's go."

Ginger and I stared at each other, then back at Lyn. He'd almost reached the front doors. I couldn't think about anything except how I'd never get my questions answered if he disappeared. "Wait," I called after him. "Lyn? Wait." But he strolled into the library without turning around.

"Something goin' on?" Ben asked.

I had no idea how to answer, and no time to come up with a convincing lie. I jumped up. "I gotta talk to that guy before we leave."

"Who is he?"

"He knows about my daddy's plane crash."

"She don't know him," Ginger said in a real urgent whisper. "She met him online."

I wanted to throttle her. "I do so know him," I said. "He's a pilot and he's from Savannah."

Ben eyed us as if we'd both been out in the sun too long. Another few seconds and my chance would be lost forever. I darted toward the library. "Be right back."

"Hey, you hold on," Ben said in a voice that meant business. But I couldn't stop. Not when I'd come this far. I tossed a pleading look over my shoulder. "I just need a minute with him, is all."

I expected to find Lyn in the lobby, seeing as how he was only a few yards ahead of me. But he wasn't there. I hurried through the double glass doors and trotted up and down the aisles, desperate for a glimpse of that black baseball cap. I ducked in between book carts and movie racks and almost ran smack into a library lady putting magazines away. She pointed a finger at me. "You slow yourself down, young lady."

"Sorry." I forced myself to walk real calm till I rounded the next corner. I paused for a second, trying to spot where Ben and Ginger were, then zigzagged through the aisles all over again, sure I'd find Lyn on the second run. Why would he introduce himself, then disappear?

A minute or so later, Ben strode around the computers with Ginger on his heels. I stooped behind a display of newspapers and took a deep breath, not sure what my next move should be. I remembered Ginger's mention of the bathroom. Maybe Lyn was in the men's room. What in the world was I supposed to do about that one?

Then it came to me. The car. He'd said the stuff about Daddy was in his car. I rushed back out to the parking lot and over to the Thunderbird.

"Hey, there she is, Daddy," Ginger called behind me.

I was afraid to look back at Ben. "I'm coming," I called over my shoulder. "Just gotta get something out of the car."

The two of them caught up with me just as I tried to

yank open the driver's-side door. Ben grabbed my elbow. "What's gotten into you, girl? You can't just go getting into somebody's car like that."

"But he said he has some stuff in there for me about Daddy."

I tried to pull free, but Ben didn't let go. He studied me with narrowed eyes. "Now, you listen here," he said. "I haven't a clue what this is all about. But there's no way I'm letting you take something out of a stranger's car."

The Thunderbird had tinted windows, so I couldn't tell if anything was on the seat or not. But I had to know. I lunged for the door with my free hand.

Ben growled under his breath and pulled me away. Then he turned me sideways and swatted me hard across the bottom. I hadn't seen it coming and it stung like a whole hive of hornets. I choked back a cry, but the tears still jumped to my eyes.

Ben steered me away from the car and gave me a little push. "Both of you, head for the truck. Now."

Ginger whirled around and I stumbled after her, the yellow parking strips wavy and blurry at my feet.

"You okay?" Ginger whispered as she scrambled up into the cab.

"Shut up," I said, and crawled in after her. Ben pulled out of the parking space and stopped by the Thunderbird.

He jotted down the license plate number on a scrap of paper. I didn't know why and wasn't about to ask, seeing as how I'd decided never to speak to him again.

We drove through town with Ben scowling and me sniffling and Ginger stone-faced between us, her hands tucked into her lap. I figured we were headed back to their house, but Ben turned up the street to our apartment instead. Ol' Faithful was parked at the curb. Mama must've just gotten home from work.

I kept my head down as I tromped up the stairs behind Ben and Ginger. I knew this time wouldn't be anything like the day at Glen Bay. This time I'd have to explain.

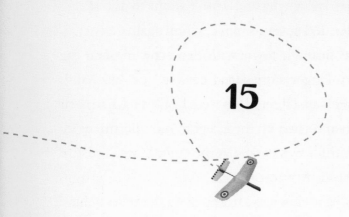

15

MAMA WAS DUSTING when we walked in. She took one look at my drippy nose and wet eyes and nearly dropped her dust rag. Her eyes swept over Ginger and then settled on Ben.

"I swatted her," he said.

"What in heavens for?"

"Better ask her."

Mama turned back to me, her eyebrows raised. "I'm listening, Piper Lee."

I had no choice but to launch into the story about Real Investigations and posting Daddy's story online and agreeing to meet Lyn. But I was careful to leave out everything

about Tina and how I'd discovered the missing-persons forum in the first place.

When I got to the part about Lyn turning out to be a
man, Mama sucked in her breath and put a hand to her
mouth. She turned and looked at Ben.

He stepped away from the wall where he'd been
leaning with his arms crossed. "I have his license plate
number. I'll call down to the prison and have 'em run
it through the computer. Should only take a few minutes."

Mama didn't say anything, just watched him walk into
the kitchen. Then she turned back to me. "What in the
world is wrong with you, Piper Lee? Surely you know better than to give private information to a complete stranger
like that?"

"But he didn't seem like a stranger, Mama. He knew
about Daddy."

"What exactly did he know?"

"He knew all about the plane crash. He remembered
it, and he even has a friend who works for the coast guard
who was there at the site."

Mama shook her head. "Honey, anybody who reads
the newspaper or knows how to search the Internet could
find out all about your daddy's plane crash. It's public

record. You can't automatically believe everything a person tells you, 'specially a stranger."

"You think he was lying? Why would he do that?"

"People lie on the Internet all the time," Ginger said, sounding like a real expert. "My teacher taught us that in third grade."

I'd almost forgotten she was in the room. It was the first word she'd spoken since we'd come back to the apartment.

Mama fixed her with a look. "Then if you knew that, I guess it was your responsibility to tell your daddy, now, wasn't it?"

Ginger paled. She opened her mouth as if she were going to say something, then stayed quiet. It made me feel just a pinch better.

"But Mama," I said, "I didn't give out a lot of private information, not even my phone number."

"But you agreed to meet him all by yourself."

"Only 'cause I thought *he* was a *she*."

"Would it have made any difference, Piper Lee? Are you honestly telling me you wouldn't have gone if you'd known he was a man?" I didn't have to think long to know she was right, and it pretty much left me at a loss for words. My silence seemed to fire her up all the more. "And who gave you permission to ride to the library by your lonesome, anyhow? I don't recall giving it."

"Miss Claudia knew 'bout it."

"And I bet she figured you'd already asked me."

"Not sure," I said.

"Well, don't worry. I intend to talk with her about it."

Ben stepped back into the living room.

"Well?" Mama said, not sounding too sure she wanted an answer.

"The car's registered to a Nathaniel Markham."

"Who's that?" Ginger said. "The guy we met said his name was Lyn." She looked at me. "Right, Piper Lee?"

"Well, yeah," I said, but I wasn't so sure what I knew anymore.

Ben sighed. He ran a hand through his hair. "Listen, you two," he said, slowing his words down as if he were talking to five-year-olds. "It means his name isn't Lyn. His name is Nathaniel Markham. He didn't want you to know his real name 'cause he was pulling the wool over your eyes. He told you he knew something about your dad, Piper Lee, so you'd agree to meet with him. And the reason he took off like he did is on account of me showin' up."

Mama stood and started to pace. "Do you have any

145

idea what could have happened to you girls? Any idea at all?"

Ben reached out to put an arm around her as she started her third lap around the room. She stunned all of us by slapping his hands away. "How could you leave the girls alone with a strange man?"

Ben's eyes sparked with surprise. "I didn't leave 'em alone with anybody, Heather."

"But you weren't there when this . . . this Lyn showed up. Were you?"

"I was at the auto-parts store."

"That's what I mean. You left them alone."

"I wasn't gone more than twenty minutes at most." Ben shook his head. "I'm sorry, Heather. You know I'd have never left 'em if I'd had a clue as to what was going on."

"But how could they plan something like this and you not know anything about it?"

Ben turned his palms up. "Now, that's a real good question. But I think you're askin' the wrong person."

Mama glanced over at me and I tried my best to look innocent. I had no idea why her anger had turned from me to Ben as fast as you'd toss a hot potato, but I figured I'd better take advantage while I could. My wide-eyed look must've worked, because Mama whirled back on Ben. "But you're the adult!" she cried.

"That don't make me a mind reader."

"I don't expect you to be a mind reader. But I do expect you to know what's going on when I leave Piper Lee with you."

"I didn't have reason to suspect anything was going on, Heather. Did you?"

"Well, maybe if you'd been paying more attention instead of worrying so much about your car, you would've noticed."

Ben studied her through narrowed eyes. The muscle in his jaw started flexing back and forth. "I wasn't worried about my car in the least," he said, his words slow and deliberate. "The girls asked if they could look around at the library for a bit, so I figured it'd be a good time to run and grab some carburetor fluid. You're making me out to be the bad guy here, and I don't see how I did anything wrong."

"But think what could've happened. What if you'd been gone even five minutes longer?"

"What's the point in letting your imagination worry you 'bout something that never happened?"

"Don't you tell me what to worry about." Mama's voice was rising.

Ben sighed. He cleared his throat. "All right, now," he said. "You got a right to be scared. I guess you even got some right to be mad at me. But you're working yourself up into a lather for nothin'.""

Mama crossed her arms. She gave Ben a good long glare before turning to me. "Piper Lee, you and Ginger go to your room for a few minutes and give us a chance to talk."

Ginger and I glanced at each other and then at Mama. Ginger probably looked at her daddy, too. But I didn't. I was too scared to look at Ben.

Ginger followed me to my bedroom and nudged the door shut with her foot. She dropped down onto the bed next to Mowgli and flicked his ear with her finger. He opened sleepy eyes and gave her an evil stare.

"Better watch it," I warned. "You'll make him mad."

She shrugged. "Everybody else is."

I couldn't argue with that one. I slumped across the foot of the bed, letting my top half hang down, the blood running to my head. I'd never expected Mama to end up more upset with Ben than with me. For a few minutes I'd been thankful, even happy. But now I felt more guilty than glad, and my heart was pulsing hard enough for me to feel the beats.

"They've never fought like this," Ginger said.

"I know."

"I hate it. It makes my stomach ache."

"Yeah," I said.

With the door closed and the fan humming, I couldn't make out exactly what was being said, but there was a whole lot of hurt leaking through the walls. Listening to it did more than make my belly ache. It made me want to cry.

Finally, after what seemed like a whole month, the bedroom door swung open and Ben said, "Ginger, let's go."

Ginger popped up like a jack-in-the-box without even a look at me. A few seconds later there came the slam of the apartment door . . . and then silence.

I crept out of my room and peeked into the living room. At first I didn't see Mama, but then I caught a glimpse of her green tank top at the kitchen window. She stood with her back to me, her forehead against the glass, her arms pulled tightly across her front. I'd never seen someone look so wilted and still be on her feet.

"Mama?" I said. "You all right?"

She didn't turn around, but she raised her head. Then she fumbled with a tissue and blew her nose two times, hard, before turning to face me. Her eyes seemed shrunk up and her cheeks were a lot redder than normal. "Oh, Piper Lee," she said. "Do you know what could've happened to you?"

"I wouldn't have gone anywhere with him, Mama. I'm not that dumb. I just wanted to find out what he knew about Daddy, is all."

"Why didn't you tell me what you were doing?"

I thought that was a pretty silly question. "'Cause I didn't figure you'd let me talk with a stranger."

Mama crossed her arms. "So how did you know you'd be able to get to the library to meet with him?"

"I didn't. Ben wanted to work on his car. He only took us 'cause Ginger and I told him I had some overdue books."

"So you lied to him?"

"I had to."

"No, you didn't have to. You chose to."

"Yes, ma'am."

Mama shook her head and took a trembly breath. "You know what I really want to know, Piper Lee? I wanna know just how you found that Real Investigations website."

My heart sank. "How I found it?"

"Yes. And there's no need for you to repeat my questions."

"It was just a pop-up."

"And where exactly were you when it popped up?"

It felt awful to have Mama glare at me that way. It hurt,

just like a bright spotlight hurts your eyes. I didn't know what to do or say. I swallowed, and even that hurt, because my throat was as rough and cracked as old pavement. I started to cry.

Mama didn't say a word. She didn't move a muscle. She just stood there and studied me. After a while she stepped across to the box of tissues on the kitchen counter, brought one over to me, and said, "Well?"

I blew my nose, and then I said, "I was trying to find Tina's phone number for Ginger."

Mama's only response was to flinch. But there was something heartbreaking in that little jump.

"Sometimes Ginger talked about her mama," I said. "She always wondered why she left and where she was now, so I thought, I just thought . . . if I could find the number . . ."

"So that's how Tina found out about the wedding." Mama gazed up at the ceiling. Then she walked out to the living room, dropped down onto the couch, and buried her face in her hands.

My heart cramped. I grabbed the box of tissues and ran to sit beside her. "I'm sorry, Mama," I whispered. "I'm sorry, I'm sorry."

Mama cried into her hands for an eternity, her

shoulders shaking up and down. And I sat there and cried with her, because what else was there for me to do?

Finally, Mama raised her head, yanked another tissue from the box, and turned to me. "Piper Lee, do you honestly think you're the only person in this world who matters?"

With all my heart I wanted to say no. But I couldn't get my tongue to form even a little word like that one.

Mama shook her head and shuddered. Then she took hold of my chin. "Now, you listen up, Piper Lee. You listen up good, because I've had enough. The Good Book says there's a time for everything, even a time to let go of things. And this is the time to let go of your daddy once and for all. So you let go of all that sadness and all that anger and whatever else you got inside of you. You hear me? You pull it all outta there and you let it go for good, just like I had to. Because your daddy's gone and he's not coming back and I can't take this anymore."

Mama released my chin and her shoulders drooped. I tried to make sense of what she'd said, especially that part about being angry. "You were mad at Daddy?" I asked.

"You bet I was mad. He's the one who made the decision to go out in the storm that day. He's the one who broke every safety rule he'd ever been taught."

I couldn't believe what I was hearing. Deep down, I'd always felt angry at Daddy for leaving us the way he had. But I'd thought I had no right. And I'd thought it was just me. Everything seemed still. Like the room, even the whole building, was holding its breath.

"Anyway," Mama said, her voice quiet. "After a while I realized that the same traits that made your daddy go out that day were the traits that made me love him so. And I knew I had to forgive him and move on. 'Cause when someone you love dies, it's your job to keep on living. That doesn't mean forgetting. He'll always be in my heart, and yours, too. But you gotta let go now. You hear?"

I nodded and grabbed another tissue. "I'm real sorry I made you and Ben fight. When are you gonna tell him about what I did with Tina?"

Mama gave a little shrug. "I'm not sure," she said. "We've decided it might be best to stop seeing each other."

I nearly came right up off the couch. "W-what?"

Mama looked at me with sad, heavy eyes. "Well," she said softly, "it's what you wanted . . . isn't it?"

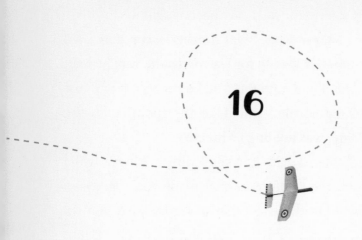

16

I WAS STRUCK still. With all the time I'd spent thinking about Mama and Ben breaking up, never once had I stopped to guess what it might actually feel like. And it felt as though I'd stepped off a cliff into a deep, black hole.

Mama pushed herself up from the couch. "I'm goin' to bed," she said.

It was all I could do to breathe as she shuffled across the rug to her bedroom and clicked the door shut behind her. It was only seven thirty.

Fresh tears overflowed and ran down my cheeks. I shook my head even though there wasn't anybody to shake it at. Nothing felt right. Not in all my ten years had Mama gone to bed before me. I always went first. And then she'd come in and pat my head and kiss me and tell me she loved me.

My mind slipped from Mama to Ben to Ginger to Lyn to Daddy in a circle that spun round and round and round again, until I felt as if I might throw up. Finally, I couldn't stand it a second longer.

I tiptoed to Mama's bedroom door and opened it a crack. There was enough light for me to see her curled on her side, a lonely hump under her navy blue sheet.

I went and kneeled on the floor next to her, and she opened her eyes. "Mama," I whispered. "You gotta talk to Ben. You gotta tell him this is all my fault and not his. Then he won't be mad at you anymore and everything will be okay."

"It's not that simple. Not for grownups."

"Then tell me how to fix things. Tell me what to do."

Mama sighed. "Mistakes are tricky things, Piper Lee. Sometimes they're easy to fix. But sometimes there's nothing you can do."

I'd thought I was all cried out, but the tears sprang up again. "No," I said. "There's gotta be a way to fix things. You just have to help me figure it out."

Mama closed her eyes. "I don't wanna talk right now, Piper Lee. Just go on to bed and get some rest. Tomorrow's another day."

So I went to bed, but I sure didn't get any rest. I cuddled beside Mowgli, with the sheet pulled over my head and my mind twirling like a Ferris wheel.

I thought about Daddy. I *did* feel angry at him for dying. But hearing Mama admit she'd felt the same way was a relief. And I thought about Lyn, about who he really was. It gave me goose bumps, lying there in the dark, and I was real glad I'd agreed to meet him at the library and not given out my home address.

I remembered how excited I'd been when I'd stumbled onto the Real Investigations website. But I hadn't heard from a single person who knew anything about Daddy. Except, of course, for Lyn, who really didn't know anything about him either. And I had to admit, deep inside, that what Mama had been telling me all along was probably right. That Daddy really, truly was gone.

And the longer I thought about it, the madder I got, because it really had been Daddy's decision to go up that day. And I felt myself start to let him slip away. And I cried some more. And when my anger finally cried itself out, and I thought just maybe I'd be able to sleep, I threw back the sheet instead. Because I knew it was up to me to fix things for Mama.

I turned on the light and got out a pencil and paper, sat on the floor, and started to write. And as the night wore on, I scribbled and erased and wrote again. And each time the words came out wrong, I quietly crumpled the paper into a ball and started over, until I'd finally written something that I prayed was good enough.

Dear Ben,

I know you're all riled up at me. You got plenty of good reasons to be riled at me, and now I'm gonna give you one more. But I hope you'll still read this letter, because it's taken a long time to write. (It's almost two in the morning and I started a long time ago.) It's my fault Tina has been bugging you. I'm the one who told her about you and Mama getting married. I found her number online. I did it a little bit for Ginger but mostly for me. (Please don't be mad at Ginger. It was my idea.) I thought if you and Tina got back together, then someday if Daddy came back, he and Mama could get back together, too. But now I know that's not gonna happen. And I know it was wrong to think that way and to do what I did. I'm real sorry.

I'm also sorry I made you and Mama fight. She wasn't really mad at you. She was just worried about me. She's been doing a lot of crying since you left. Me too. (And I don't usually cry very much.)

Please don't be so mad at me that you're mad at Mama, too. So I hope you will do two things for me. One: call Mama and tell her everything will be okay. She believes the stuff you tell her. Please do it soon. And two: give me one more chance. I am very, very sorry. I promise to be a better kid from now on.

Love, Piper Lee

P.S. Mama did not make me write this. She don't know about it.

There was one fat tear mark on the bottom of the page. I tried to rub it away, but it smudged and looked even worse. I folded the letter anyway, stuffed it into an envelope, and licked the seal real quick before I could change my mind.

But as soon as I did that, it dawned on me that the letter might take two days to reach Ben. And I knew I'd never survive two whole days of suspense. I wasn't sure my nerves could take another five minutes. I started to panic, because the only faster thing was to call him, and there was no way I could do that. I'd never be able to think of what to say.

But then I realized I had the words right in my hand. I tore the envelope open and pulled out the paper. Then

I crept through the dark living room to the phone in the kitchen. I switched on the little bulb above the stove so I'd have enough light to read by.

Ben didn't answer until the sixth ring, and his voice was so thick with sleep that it didn't even sound like him.

"Ben?"

"Who's this?" he mumbled.

"It's me," I said. "Piper Lee. I'm real sorry to wake you up."

"Piper Lee? You know what time it is?"

"Yes, sir. It's two o'clock. But I wrote a letter to you, and it's real important. Will you listen?"

"Right now?"

"It won't take long."

He paused and then moaned. "Okay," he said.

So I rambled through the letter, and when I got to the end, I just stopped. I couldn't think of anything more to say.

"That it?" Ben asked.

"That's it."

"All right, then. Go on back to bed now."

I wanted to ask what he thought, if he'd agree to call Mama, if he'd give me one more chance. But I didn't have the courage to ask anything. "Okay," I whispered. "Thanks for listening." And I clicked off the light and tiptoed back to bed and to Mowgli and pulled the sheet up over us both.

I slept clear through till nine the next morning. Then I lay there for another half hour listening to the sounds of Mama moving around the kitchen and the clackity-clack of Miss Claudia's sewing machine. But when the phone rang, my heart about stopped, and I hightailed it to my doorway in time to watch Mama pick up.

I knew it was Ben by the way her face got hard but her eyes got soft. "I'm fine," she said, hesitating a little, as if she couldn't quite decide if she should try to sound mad or happy or neither one. "She did?" she said a minute later. "No. Well, I don't know. Maybe. Well . . . I s'pose it couldn't hurt."

I couldn't quite guess the conversation by the little bits of words I heard and the long pauses in between, but my imagination was sure going crazy.

"She's still in bed," Mama said. She glanced toward my room and our eyes met. "Oh, she is up . . . Hold on." She held out the phone and said, "Ben wants to talk to you."

I swallowed. "He does?" My heart started to pound and my hands turned sticky and cold. "Okay," I said. I forced myself to take the phone. "Hello."

Ben cleared his throat. "Mornin', Piper Lee. I was half-asleep last night, but I wanted you to know I was listening."

"Oh . . . okay."

"I 'preciate the effort."

"Okay," I repeated.

"I took tomorrow afternoon off for the air show," he said. "But instead of doin' that, we're gonna get together and have a talk. Iron some things out . . . all four of us."

"Yes, sir," I said, and nearly crumpled with relief that it would be all of us and not just him and me.

"All right, then," he said. "Bye, now."

And that was it. I put the phone down. I'd honestly forgotten about the air show, but now I looked at Mama and started to cry. "He said we have to talk tomorrow instead of goin' to the air show."

Mama nodded. "So he did."

I fell into her arms, and she smoothed down my hair. "So you called him, huh? How come you did that?"

"To try to fix things."

"Brave girl," she said, and I could almost hear a smile in her voice. "I'm proud of you for trying."

"Did it work?"

"I'm not sure. We both said some pretty hurtful things to each other."

"Then you both need to apologize," I said. "That's what you always tell me."

"Just whose side are you on, anyway?"

I sniffled against her shoulder. "I'm scared about tomorrow. About what he's gonna say to me."

Mama's chest rose and fell with her sigh. "It'll be okay, Piper Lee." But I thought she sounded a little scared herself. "Ginger's coming over tomorrow morning," she added. "I guess her regular sitter has the flu."

"Oh," I said.

She held me away from her and smiled. "Look at that hair of yours. How 'bout if you go pull it back outta your face and I make us some breakfast?"

The day was long and slow. I stayed in my pajamas until noon and then took a long bath. The evening wasn't much better. Mama and I didn't talk much. We sat on the couch and watched an old Western on TV, but I spent most of the time nibbling my thumbnail and staring off into space. All I could think about was tomorrow, and the big talk, and just how much trouble I was in with Ben, and about whether he and Mama would end up back together or not.

Finally I told Mama my belly didn't feel too good. She put the back of her hand on my forehead and shook her head. "You're not sick," she said. "You're just worried." She brought me a glass of ginger ale to sip on, then held out her arms. I scooted over and laid my head on her shoulder until it was time for bed.

I lay in the dark, looking out at the smidgen of sky I could see through my window and thinking about Daddy. And that made me feel better than anything else could.

I slept even longer the next morning, and when I finally shuffled out to the kitchen in my pajamas, I was surprised to find Ginger already there.

"Hey, Piper Lee," she said. "Didn't think you were ever gonna get up."

I rubbed my eyes. "What time you get here?"

"I dunno. Eight thirty or so."

Mama stirred some sugar into a gallon jug of water and then dropped six tea bags over the rim before screwing on the lid. "You were sawin' logs pretty good when I checked on you a bit ago," she said.

Ginger wore a purple T-shirt and a ruffly pink skirt. The necklace from Tina hung down her front. I went back to my room to get dressed and pulled my hair back into a ponytail.

"Aren't you even gonna brush it?" Ginger asked.

I turned to see her standing in the doorway, her hands on her hips.

"You're s'posed to knock," I said.

"Brushing your hair makes it look shiny," she told me.

"I don't care. And knock before you waltz in."

"Hey, Piper, can we go fly your glider plane for a while?"

Her question gave me a little pinging feeling in my heart. Today was the air show and I wouldn't be there. I didn't especially want to think about planes right then. "No," I said. "Not now."

"Then what do you wanna do?"

"Eat breakfast," I said. But I only said it to shut her up, as food wasn't too high on my list of wants right then either.

Mama gave me half a grapefruit and a piece of toast. After that she handed me the gallon jug of tea and told us to go put it outdoors in the sun. I carried it out back and set it among Miss Claudia's flowers. Then Ginger and I plopped down onto the cement steps.

The sun was good and warm, but not too hot yet. Bees hummed around the bachelor's buttons, and purple spikes of lavender swayed in the breeze. The whole backyard smelled like a perfume factory.

I clasped my hands around my knees and gave Ginger a sideways glance. She tried to reach one of Miss Claudia's cherry tomatoes without falling off the step. "So," I said, "did you know I called your daddy?"

Ginger picked the tomato and popped it into her mouth with a look of triumph. "Yeah, we talked all about it."

"He told you what I said?"

She shook her head. "Said it was just between the two of you."

"Oh." I felt a warm rush of thankfulness.

"You sure I can't fly your glider? Just for a bit?"

I sighed. What difference did it make? "Okay, I guess. It's upstairs in my top dresser drawer."

She hopped up. "All righty. Be right back."

"Yeah," I said. "And don't you dare touch anything else in my room, you hear me?"

I glanced up at all the obstacles that my plane could crash into. Trees and electric poles and rooftops, not to mention the apartment building itself.

"Aim it that way," I directed when Ginger came back a minute later. "And if you land it in a tree, you gotta climb up and rescue it."

Giving orders to Ginger gave me something to do, and watching the plane perform its graceful swoops and arcs made me feel a tiny bit better. But I couldn't quit worrying over what Ben was gonna say or do about all the trouble I'd caused. And as the sun moved higher in the sky and the tea turned a dark amber, I knew it must be getting on to noon. "So, was your daddy put-out with you for callin' your mama?" I asked.

"No."

"Well . . . is he really put-out with me for giving you the number?"

"Well, 'course. Wouldn't you be if you were him?"

And that was all it took to flip my stomach inside out.

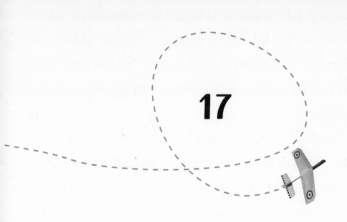

17

BEN STILL HADN'T shown up by one o'clock. I sat on the living room rug and tried to coax Mowgli into batting his catnip mouse while Ginger watched *Little House on the Prairie*. I would've given my two front teeth to know what Ben was going to do so I could at least prepare for it.

Would he and Mama get in another fight? Would he yell at me? Would he punish me? He probably figured I deserved a licking. Would Mama let him do it? A trickle of sweat ran down my back.

Mama flitted from room to room without seeming to do anything. She scrubbed the kitchen table with a dish-rag and then five minutes later scrubbed it again.

The phone jangled at one twenty-four.

I held my breath as Mama answered it. But after "Hello," she didn't say anything more, just stood there with a funny look on her face. Her eyes widened as she listened, and her breathing got faster. "All right . . . thank you," she said. She set the phone down. "Turn to channel four."

Ginger glanced over from the TV. "Do what?"

"Channel four," Mama snapped. "Now."

I'd never heard Mama use that voice with her. Ginger jumped up and grabbed the remote off the coffee table.

The screen changed to a man wearing a headset microphone. A banner at the bottom of the TV scrolled LIVE — GEORGIA DEPARTMENT OF CORRECTIONS FACILITY, and in the background towered the gray stone walls of the prison where Ben worked.

"First of all, Karen," the reporter said, "this facility is divided into three general areas, or blocks, referred to as J-block, C-block, and L-block, and only C-block is involved in this disturbance. So far, all we know is that when this incident began, approximately three hundred inmates who reside in C-block were in the yard as part of their regular Saturday activities. About ten thirty, an officer's body alarm sounded in C-block, indicating that an officer was down. Several others responded to the distress call and were confronted by a group of inmates, who overpowered some of the officers."

Mama sucked in her breath.

I kept my eyes on the reporter.

"At the same time, in the areas where these officers had previously been, the inmates left their housing units and moved up to the C-block corridor. Although the details are hazy at this time, Karen, we do have reports of at least two injured guards and several injured inmates. The prison has been placed on lockdown and will remain that way throughout the disturbance."

Ginger let out a yelp. "Daddy!" she cried.

Mama's face was the color of a mushroom.

I turned back to the TV and heard a woman's voice ask, "Is there any indication as to what might have triggered this disturbance, Charlie?"

"Well, nothing concrete at this point, Karen. But we do know that the Georgia legislature has recently slashed funding for many popular inmate programs, such as college accreditation courses and many sports programs, and there's been a lot of dissention and unrest because of it. So that's a likely possibility."

"My God," Mama whispered. "Ben was right."

I was about to ask, *Right about what?* But as soon as I opened my mouth, Mama put a finger to her lips and pointed back at the TV.

"So what is the plan at this point?" Karen asked.

"Well," Charlie said, "correctional professionals know that, unlike movie portrayals where a massive show of force is used to overwhelm the bad guys, disturbances such as this one are most often resolved through patient negotiation and interagency cooperation. Local law-enforcement agencies are providing perimeter security at this time, and a command center has been set up by officials of the Georgia Department of Corrections."

The reporter paused and looked down at some papers in his hand.

"Apparently the governor has placed the National Guard on standby, but as the governor indicated, his primary mission is the preservation of life and to bring a quick and peaceful end to this disturbance. We'll certainly keep you updated as events unfold. Charlie Gallagher, reporting live for News 4."

Ginger got up and stumbled toward Mama. "Is Daddy okay, Heather? What did they say?"

Mama opened her arms to Ginger. "I'm sure he's fine, honey."

I pictured Ben, how he'd moved those heavy railroad ties around by himself when we'd made the garden. Of course he'd be fine.

"What does *lockdown* mean?" I asked.

"It means nobody is allowed to go in or out," Mama said.

"For how long?"

"Until the officers get control again, I s'pose."

"Heather," Ginger whispered, "I'm worried about Daddy."

Mama blinked very fast and smoothed Ginger's hair.

"What are we gonna do?" I said.

"The officer on the phone said we're s'posed to go to the Creston High School gym," Mama answered. "They've set it up for the families so they can keep everyone updated at the same time."

None of us spoke the whole ten-minute ride across town. Mama gripped the steering wheel and stared out through the light rain pattering the windshield. Ginger sniffled. I didn't know what to do. One thing was for sure, though—I could quit worrying about our big talk.

Creston High School was an old, red brick building that looked as though it had been there since the Civil War. Cars filled the parking lot and spilled out onto the grassy areas bordering the side streets. We parked and headed for the main entrance.

People darted around inside, talking on cell phones or clomping up and down the bleachers. Mama searched the crowd, looking lost. Finally she steered us over to the far side of the gym and we sat down on some bleachers, next to a blond lady with a baby on her lap.

The lady gave Mama a nervous smile. "I'm Patty Patella. My husband, John, works as a guard."

"Your baby's cute as a button," Mama said. "How old is he?"

The lady's eyes filled with tears. "Fourteen months. And I just found out this morning I'm pregnant again. Can y'all believe it? I haven't even gotten to tell John yet."

Mama reached over and gave Patty's hand a squeeze as though she'd known her a long time.

After we'd been there a half hour or so, a man with a microphone walked to the center of the gym. He wore tan pants and a dress shirt with the sleeves rolled up to his elbows. He blew into the microphone, and the harsh hissing grabbed everyone's attention.

"Ladies and gentlemen," he said. "My name is Carl Stevens. I'm the assistant director of the Georgia Department of Corrections. Thank you for being willing to come here; I know this is an extremely stressful time. Let me start by quieting the rumor mill and giving you some basic facts.

"The disturbance began about ten this morning. A fight broke out among twelve inmates as they were being taken back inside after recreation. By the time other guards were able to respond, the fight had expanded to include roughly sixty inmates. At this point, we believe there are at least twenty guards and twenty-five inmates being held hostage."

People shouted angry questions at Mr. Stevens, like they thought the whole thing was his fault. Every time he tried to walk away, someone shouted a new question. I was glad I wasn't him. At last he raised both hands. "Ladies and gentlemen, that's all the information I have right now. The second I hear anything more, you'll hear it, too. In the meantime, help yourself to coffee and soft drinks."

Ginger's chin quivered. "If something happens to Daddy, I won't have anybody. I'll be all alone."

"Oh, honey," Mama said, "nonsense. First of all, your daddy's gonna be just fine. And you wouldn't be alone anyhow—you have me and Piper Lee."

"Not Piper Lee," Ginger said. "She doesn't want you and Daddy to get married. She probably hopes something happens to him."

I jerked back like she'd tossed me a firecracker.

173

Mama placed her hand on my knee. "She didn't mean it, Piper Lee. She's just scared."

I jumped up. "I'm gonna go get something to drink." I slipped over to the refreshment table, where two coolers overflowed with ice and drinks. I reached in for a cherry cola and then moved a few steps away. Ginger's comment burned like scalding water.

Did she truly believe I wanted something bad to happen to Ben? It wasn't true. But to have her think so made me want to shrivel up like a slug in the sun. I caught glimpses of her and Mama through gaps in the crowd. Ginger was resting her head on Mama's shoulder. I could tell she wasn't trying to win points; she was just real scared for Ben.

I took a closer look at the people around me, at the fear in their faces. Something bad really could happen inside those gray prison walls—to Patty Patella's husband, maybe even to Ben.

I finished my Coke. Then I fished a root beer out of the cooler for Ginger and filled a Styrofoam cup with coffee for Mama. She smiled when I offered it to her. "Thanks, sweetie. That was nice."

Ginger opened the root beer, took one swallow, and then set the can beside her. Patty's baby made a grab for it. "What's his name?" she asked Patty.

"Austin James."

"Could I hold him?"

Patty shifted the baby onto Ginger's lap. "He's so bored. He wants to get down and run around."

"We could walk him around," I said. "If you want us to."

She seemed relieved. "Go right ahead."

Ginger and I each took one of his fat little hands, and he grinned. But it took only a few seconds to figure out that he didn't want to hold hands—he wanted to run free. We circled him like a moving fence, trying to keep him in Patty's view. But all of a sudden he slipped free and took off in a wobbly run.

Halfway across the gym I grabbed him by the back of his overalls. He squealed as loud as a cornered hog, and a bunch of people scowled. I let go right away.

Patty came out of nowhere and scooped him up. "Thanks for trying," she said. She hurried away with Austin shrieking in her arms. Ginger stared after them.

"What?" I said.

"How old do you think Patty is?"

"I dunno. Why?"

"'Cause I was just thinking that I was about Austin's age when Mama decided to leave."

Austin's little blond head bobbed over Patty's shoulder

as she wove her way through the crowd. I tried to picture her walking out on him, saying he was just too much work. But of course she wouldn't. How could anyone?

"I think Patty's older than your mama was."

"Mama was plenty old enough," Ginger said with a spunk I hadn't heard before. "You don't have to stick up for her."

"I wasn't," I said. "I was just . . ." and then my voice trailed off. I didn't know how to explain that it was her I was trying to stick up for, not Tina.

"She called yesterday."

"How come you didn't say so before?"

Ginger shrugged. "After she finishes her travel-agent training, she wants to come see me for a couple days."

"What'd your daddy say?"

"That it's up to me."

"Well, you want her to come, don't you?"

"Maybe. I gotta think about it some."

I recalled what she'd said a minute before, about Tina being plenty old enough. "You know I don't want anything to happen to your daddy, right? I swear I never thought such a thing."

"I know," Ginger said. She rubbed at her face. "You probably think I'm acting like a baby, but it's just that I wanna see him so bad right now."

"I don't think you're being a baby." I put my hand on her shoulder. "I wouldn't mind seeing him myself."

I wish I'd had a camera to capture the look she gave me — as though for just one second she thought I was the greatest person in the whole world. It gave me enough courage to say the rest. "I should never have gotten you all excited about trying to find your mama. I'm sorry I ever started it."

"I'm not," Ginger said. "Not really. 'Cause now I don't have to wonder so much."

"You don't hate me?"

"Course not."

And then it was my turn to get choked up.

The afternoon dragged into evening. Mama and Ginger and I went outdoors and walked three laps around the high school track. It was still raining a bit, but the air was warm and smelled of damp earth and jasmine.

We went back inside, and Ginger and I ate some pepperoni pizza. Mama said she wasn't hungry and drank another cup of coffee. It was 6:35 p.m. when the sharp whine of a microphone caught our attention. The room hushed.

"Ladies and gentlemen," Mr. Stevens said, "I'm thrilled to announce the release of all of the hostages, with the exception of five inmates and five guards."

Shouts and whistles filled the air. Mama let out a happy gasp.

"Who?" somebody hollered from across the gym.

Mr. Stevens raised both arms until everybody shut up again. "I'm going to read off the names of the released guards. You can meet up with your loved ones at the Maycomb County Hospital, where they're being checked out."

Mama leaned forward between Ginger and me, holding our hands. She squeezed mine so hard that it filled with pins and needles.

Mr. Stevens held up his list. After each name he paused for what seemed like forever to allow for the ruckus as people gathered their stuff and hurried out.

Patty's husband was number nine. I smiled as she swooped up Austin's diaper bag and bent to give Mama a quick hug.

"Go," Mama whispered. "Go tell that man of yours he's gonna be a daddy again."

Patty's eyes shone. "Y'all are in my prayers."

I counted every name Mr. Stevens read.

There were seventeen.

But not one of them was Ben Hutchings.

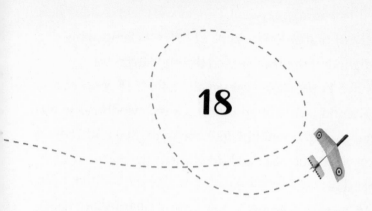

18

Mr. Stevens set down his microphone and folded the paper. The look on Mama's face ripped a hole in my chest big enough to walk through.

I put an arm around her. "It's gonna be okay," I whispered. "He'll read the other names soon. You'll see."

"Oh, Ben," Mama said. "Please don't do this to me."

I understood exactly what she was saying. She'd already lost Daddy. She couldn't stand the thought of losing another person she loved. And that's when I knew just how much she loved Ben. And I realized more than ever what a stupid thing I'd done—not just as far as Lyn, but the whole Operation Finding Tina thing. A million little needles of guilt pricked through my skin and ground their way down to my very soul. Ginger was right. I didn't have a speck of brains—or a speck of heart. I clamped my eyes real tight, but the tears leaked through anyhow.

When I opened my eyes again, a flash of color caught my attention. A woman wearing a red windbreaker was carrying a cardboard box into the gym. She pulled out a bunch of plastic bags and lined them up on the refreshment table.

Mr. Stevens scooped up an armful of bags and began making his way around the gym. Finally he came around to us and offered a tired smile. "Hello there. How are you ladies holding up?"

Mama straightened her shoulders. "We're getting by. Thank you."

He held out one of the bags. "Here's a comfort pack."

I was curious to see what was inside, but Mama didn't open it right away, so I made myself wait. Mr. Stevens dropped down onto the bleacher below us. His tie was a big, loose loop around his neck. "This is some day, isn't it? Who are you waiting for?"

"Ben Hutchings," Mama said. "He's one of the guards."

Mr. Stevens broke into a big smile. "Oh, sure. I know Ben."

Ginger perked right up. "You know my daddy?"

"Sure do. We run into each other at the snack machine quite often. Seems we both have a weakness for honey-roasted peanuts."

Ginger and Mama gave each other a knowing smile. I thought about how I didn't even know Ben liked peanuts.

"Did you see him today?" Mama asked.

"No. But I did a few days back. He said something about only working half a day today, that he had some-place to take his three favorite girls."

Had Ben truly included me right along with Mama and Ginger?

"The air show," Mama said. She touched my knee. "Piper Lee loves airplanes."

Mr. Stevens winked at me. "Well, I'm sure sorry this had to happen instead. But I bet he'll find some way to make it up to you."

"Yes, sir," I said. But I knew Ben didn't have a single thing to make up to me.

Mr. Stevens glanced at his watch. "If you decide to spend the night, there are pillows and blankets available. Or if you'd rather, you can go home, and I'll notify you of any new developments right away."

"I think we'll stay awhile yet," Mama said.

"All right. Remember, there's plenty of hot coffee over there."

"I know," Mama said. "I think I've already drunk a gallon of it."

I counted fifteen people in the gym, most sitting in quiet little groups—a lady with two teenage boys, an old couple holding hands, a woman with a little girl who looked about five years old, her hair all done up in cornrow braids.

"So what's a comfort pack?" I asked.

Mama raised her eyebrows. "Why don't you check it out for us?"

I set each item on the bench in front of us. Cherry lip balm, Kleenex, a toothbrush and tiny tube of Crest paste, a bottle of water, soap, two packs of tropical flavor Life Savers, and a deck of cards.

"Want to play crazy eights, Ginger?"

"Yeah, I guess."

Mama sipped the bottled water while Ginger and I sucked on Life Savers and played cards. After a while Mama opened the pack of Kleenex and blew her nose. Then she said, "How do you feel about spending the night?"

"I'm not leaving," Ginger said.

"Me neither," I said.

Mama seemed relieved. "Good. Then we'll stay."

It was quiet in the gym now, but my ears still hummed

from all the earlier noise. By the time we'd played our third game of crazy eights, it seemed like too much work to hold my head up.

Ginger slid the cards back into their box. I rested my feet on the bleacher below me and put my head down on my arms. Mama rubbed my back.

We all sat there, each thinking our own thoughts for a while. Then Mama yawned. "I think I'll go ask Mr. Stevens about those pillows he mentioned."

"Heather?" Ginger asked. "Do you think Daddy's scared?"

Mama gazed up at the ceiling. "I don't know, honey. I'm sure he has plenty on his mind."

"What do you think he's thinking about?"

"Us," she said. "I'll bet he's thinking 'bout us."

They smiled at each other, just like they'd smiled about the honey-roasted peanuts. I thought about the money I'd saved for the air show, and I wondered how many peanuts I could buy for thirteen dollars.

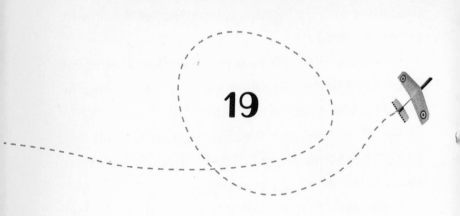

19

MR. STEVENS TURNED out some of the lights, but it didn't make it any easier to sleep. The bleachers were too hard, and my pillow slipped every time I changed position. Ginger stretched out one row above me. Mama just propped a pillow behind her back and leaned her head on one hand. Every time I opened my eyes, hers were open too.

If something happened to Ben, would Ginger stay with me and Mama? If she did, would we live in our apartment or move into Ben's house? My bedroom was pretty small, but Ginger's was big—hers would be better. I thought about what life might be like if Ben and Mama made up and got married. We'd probably go swimming a lot. Maybe Ben would cup his hands and let me step into them and toss me into the water like he did with Ginger. Then we'd go home afterward and have chicken for supper or maybe barbecue some pork.

Come fall we'd watch lots of football and eat some of the good stuff from Mama's garden — sweet corn and peas, for sure, probably tomatoes and beans, but no okra. I'd talk her out of planting okra.

Maybe Ben would finally get his old Mustang fixed up real fancy and drive it in the Fourth of July parade. Ginger and I could ride in the back and toss red-hots and root-beer barrels to all the little kids begging for candy along the sidewalk.

Mama sucked in a sharp breath, and the sound yanked me out of my daydream.

I sat up and followed her gaze to the middle of the gym, where Mr. Stevens stood grinning. He didn't even bother with the microphone this time, just waved his hands and said, "Okay, everybody. I've got some news you're all going to want to hear. I've just received word that the crisis is officially over. The rioters have been taken into custody and the hostages released. You can meet up with your loved ones at Maycomb Hospital. Please drive safely, and God bless."

The air exploded with voices crying "Praise the Lord!" and "Thank God Almighty!"

Ginger jumped off the bleachers and hopped around like some wild rabbit. "That means Daddy's okay, doesn't it, Heather? It means he's okay."

"I'm just sure of it," Mama said, "but let's go find out for ourselves."

I don't remember much about our trip to the hospital, just that it seemed to take a long time, even though it was only a couple miles away and even though Mama drove thirty-nine miles an hour instead of the twenty-five she was supposed to.

Everybody from the school got there about the same time, and a whole rush of people filled the hospital lobby. We had to wait in line before a nurse checked her charts and pointed us down the hall to room 114. Mama walked as fast as she could without running, and Ginger and I trotted along beside her.

The door to room 114 was open, and there was Ben, slumped on the side of the bed, looking dead tired. But as soon as he saw us, his whole face lit up. He made it to his feet right before Ginger flew into him with Mama half a step behind. He didn't say anything, just wrapped his arms around them and dropped his head low against Mama's.

I hovered a few steps back, feeling like a racehorse trapped behind its gate. But then Ben raised his head and said, "You get over here, Piper Lee," and I bolted over to wiggle my way in between Mama and Ginger.

The four of us stayed all locked up like that until Mama finally stepped back and noticed the gash on Ben's forehead. "Oh," she said, "your poor, poor head."

Ben smiled and gently put his hand around Mama's to keep her from touching the cut. "I told 'em I was just fine," he said. "But the nurse says I can't leave until they stitch it up."

"And your hand," Ginger said. "You hurt it, too."

Ben glanced at the dried blood on his skinned knuckles and winked at her. "Yeah, just a little, but you should see the other guy."

Ginger and I giggled, but Mama glared up at him and even stamped her foot. "Don't you dare make jokes, Ben Hutchings. Not a bit of this is funny. Not a bit. The girls and I just spent the past twelve hours terrified to death, not knowing if you . . . if we'd ever . . ." Mama's voice cracked and her words trailed off in a sob.

Ben pulled her close. "Hush now, Heather. I didn't mean it like that. And I'm real sorry about Thursday, too. You were right and I was wrong."

Mama shook her head. "No, no. I'm the sorry one. I had no right to blame you for something outta your control."

"Does that mean the wedding's back on?" Ben asked.

"I'd sure like it to be," Mama said.

Ginger bumped me with her elbow and pointed to the clock. "Looky there. It's one in the morning. I've never gotten to stay up this late before." Then she yawned, and that got me doing the same thing. I went and curled up in one of the padded chairs over by the window.

Mama sat on the bed with Ben, clinging to his hand as though she never planned to let go. Ginger sat on his other side and asked a bunch of questions about the riot. Ben wouldn't say much about what had happened inside the prison, but when Ginger mentioned Mr. Stevens and the honey-roasted peanuts, he chuckled and said, "Yeah, that Carl's a good guy."

Then all of a sudden he looked over at me and said, "We never got to have that talk of ours, did we?"

I tensed up and bowed my head. "No, sir. I guess not."

"Well, we still can," Mama said. "How 'bout tomorrow?"

"I got a better idea," Ben said, looking at Mama. "Let's forget the talk and get married tomorrow instead."

I snapped my head up, sure I'd heard him wrong. But the way Ginger's mouth dropped open told me I'd heard right.

Mama grinned. She shook her head. "Tomorrow? Have you lost your marbles? We can't get married tomorrow."

Ben's eyes crinkled at the corners. "Why not? You just told me the wedding was back on. If not tomorrow, how 'bout next Saturday?"

"But . . . but the date's all set."

"Heather DeLuna, are you gonna marry me or not? 'Cause if you are, I don't wanna wait another month."

Mama searched his face. "But that don't give me enough time."

"Time for what? You and the girls have your dresses. We got the rings. The guests can take pictures for us."

"But the cake," Mama said. "And the flowers."

"I can make the cake," Ginger piped up. "Any kind you like, Heather. I can make a real good chocolate cake."

"And I know where there's a bunch of flowers," I said, unable to resist the sudden excitement swooping around the room. "Miss Claudia won't mind a bit if we pick 'em."

Mama shook her head. She put her fingertips to her temples. "I believe you've all lost your marbles," she said. Then she looked from one to the other of us and started to laugh. "Y'all are serious, aren't you ?. . . It won't be much of a wedding."

"All the wedding I need," Ben said. And he took

Mama's face in his hands and started kissing her. And it was the most disgusting thing, because they were still kissing when the nurse came in to stitch up Ben's cut.

"Well, now," she said when she came into the room and caught them. "I was gonna apologize for makin' you wait, but it seems you didn't mind so much."

"No, ma'am," Ben said. "Not at all."

The nurse smiled around the room at each of us. I knew she thought that Mama and Ben were husband and wife and that me and Ginger were their kids. But I smiled back at her anyhow, and it made me feel good, because I felt sure Daddy wouldn't mind. After all, I'd always be his daughter; I'd always love him. But that didn't mean I couldn't be part of something new.

20

Saturday dawned clear and bright and sticky hot. Mama and Ben decided to get married in Charlesburg Park, seeing as how the church wasn't available on such short notice. My yellow dress pinched at the waist and prickled at the neck, and the stiff netting made my legs itch. But Miss Claudia made me laugh when she gave me a secret wink and said, "Why, Piper Lee. I believe you've got the prettiest dress I've ever laid eyes on."

Ginger didn't seem bothered by her dress in the least. Her bra caused a slight ripple in the material, and I hoped my new bra caused a ripple, too, but Ginger never gave me the chance to ask. She pranced around the guests like some hired hostess, handing out construction-paper fans and thanking everyone for coming.

But it was Mama who stole the show in her beautiful peach dress with white eyelet trim, her hair all loose and flowing around her shoulders like a cloud. I'd never seen her smile so big. And I even had to admit that Ben looked pretty sharp in his dark blue suit.

Some of the workers from the prison showed up, including Mr. Stevens, who surprised Mama and Ben with a brand-new digital camera for wedding pictures. Ben stopped Ginger and me from fighting over it by saying she could take pictures during the ceremony but I got it for the reception. But when it came time for Mama and Ben to cut into the sloping, slightly melted chocolate cake, Ginger still hadn't handed it over.

"I made the cake," she said, "so I should get to take the first picture of them eatin' it."

"I don't care who made it," I snapped. "It's the reception, and you're s'posed to give me a turn."

"I'll give it over in a few minutes." She scooted behind the beverage table for a better shot.

I scooted right after her. "You'll give it now." I made a grab for it.

And right as Mama put the first bit of cake into Ben's

mouth and all the guests clapped and cheered, the camera slipped from my fingers and splashed right into the bowl of lemon-lime punch. I fished it out of there before you could say "Jack Sprat," but Ginger still screamed.

"Shut up," I hissed. "I got it."

"You probably ruined that brand-new camera!" she cried.

"Did not ruin it." I gave the camera a good shake and then toweled it off real careful with the hem of my dress.

"I'm telling, Piper Lee. I bet it don't work anymore."

"I grabbed it out plenty fast," I said. "Don't be a tattle-tale."

She put her hands on her hips, and I could see her weighing her options. A smug little grin spread across her face. "Are you offerin' me something if I keep quiet?"

I rolled my eyes. "Ginger, sometimes you are such a pain in the petunia." I glanced over at Mama and Ben. Ben was playing around, holding a bite of cake right near Mama's mouth before pulling it back again, and everyone was laughing. Everything was so perfect, I couldn't bear the thought of having either one of them mad at me. "I dunno," I said. "What do you want?"

Ginger pursed her lips and rocked back and forth on her shiny white shoes. "Top bunk for a month."

I narrowed my eyes. Ben had put up a brand-new set of bunk beds in Ginger's bedroom. We'd played penny poker to decide who got the top bunk for the first month, and I'd won. "Go tattle if you want," I said. "But there's no way you're getting it that long."

"Well, not for the whole month, then. Two weeks— how's that?"

"Ten days," I said. "Ten days only. And if you don't give it up the second you're s'posed to, I'll throw you off."

"Fine," she said. "Ten days. Now I'm gonna go get Mama to cut me a piece of cake." And she whirled around and flounced off.

I sighed. I was pretty sure this was what having Ginger for a sister would be like—plenty of battles, plenty of bickering, and plenty of standing my ground when I really had to.

I watched Ginger hop up behind Mama and grab her around the waist. She'd started calling her "Mama" even before the wedding vows had been said, and I knew there wasn't any point in correcting her now. I figured I'd keep calling Ben by his regular name. Calling him "Daddy" just wouldn't feel right on my tongue, and I didn't know if he'd want me to anyhow. Maybe "Dad" would be okay someday. But for now "Ben" would do just fine.

I finished patting off the camera and gave it a careful look. It was dry now, and the open and close button worked just fine. Why hadn't I checked it out before giving up the top bunk? I clicked a picture of Ben wiping a drip of frosting from Mama's chin and another of the big bouquet of lavender we'd set up next to the guest book. Then Miss Claudia filled the viewing window in her billowing blue skirt, and I clicked a picture of her horrified look as she spied the big wet punch stains all over my dress.

"Lordy, child," she said. "I'm not even gonna ask."

"Good." I grinned. "'Cause I really don't wanna say."

Miss Claudia put her hands on her chest and laughed in her loud, joyous way, and I laughed, too. Then I glanced over at Mama and Ben and Ginger standing by the cake table. Mama held out a little paper plate and waved for me to come. And I ran over to get my own piece of sloping, slightly melted chocolate cake.

Acknowledgments

The publication of this book is the end result of eight years of effort. Not just on my part, but on the part of my agent, Mary Kole, who had not only the faith to sign me on but also the skill and determination to sell my book. Thanks, Mary!

I'm also indebted to the hardworking Harcourt gang who made my first experience with publication such a wonderful one. Special thanks to my editor, Adah Nuchi, whose skillful direction elevated this book from good to great.

Thanks also to the Sandpoint branch of the Idaho Writers League who patiently listened to and made suggestions on the early drafts.

And finally, a hug of appreciation to my husband, Ted, and my daughter, Adriana, who don't seem to object to me hogging the computer. I love you guys!